something barely remembered

For Esther and Mariam, remembering Paul

contents

Lukose's church

My mother gave birth to me in a small room at the back of the house. The midwife was an old woman with a moustache, her hands gnarled but steady. She cut the cord with which mother and I had been linked with a flat heavy iron knife. It had no handle, and I would often look at it with dread, as it hung on the wall by two small holes inserted into nails. I had seen it cut off the heads of chickens when guests came, or at Christmas – a nonchalance of chopping which was repeated on raw mangoes, plantains, jackfruit. I had seen it, as a boy, being dipped into boiling water and taken in to my mother and her second son, so that the midwife could sever them too. Above the knife hung the fishing rods, and the long bamboo poles which mother used to knock down tamarind pods, guavas for us, and the raw mangoes she used in cooking.

I was the first son, and they named me after my paternal grandfather Lukose. My mother often told me that when I was born she was afraid, because she thought she had given birth to Grandfather – my eyes were clear and open, brown and unglazed. She said that I looked at her at the very moment of my birth and that there was a perfect understanding of her. I think it was her preoccupation with Grandfather and my resemblance to him that always created an intangible distance between us. She was always affectionate, but almost deferential, and she never held me close to her as she did my younger brother Behnan. It was not surprising then that when I took on ordainment and became a priest as my grandfather and his father, and his father before him had been, she began to call me Achen, Father – and it seemed the most natural thing that I should once more be severed, not by the spatulate kitchen knife, but by an equally blunt act of deference by mother.

I grew up by the River Pamba. It was broad and still, and its face was different from morning to evening. Kingfishers flew low across, their wings taking on the colours of sky, light and water. Across, on the other side were the green fields of paddy. And at the edge of the river were the swaying reed-like silhouettes of sugar cane which reflected themselves dark and ominous in the water. On our side of the river there were some large rocks, sand, and that beautiful wild plant which we call *thotta vadi* – touch-and-it-will-wilt. I spent many hot and lazy afternoons on the banks watching the kingfishers and waiting for mother to call.

I don't know when it was that I received the calling. Perhaps it was that day when I felt the sun burn into my blood, and yet my head was filled with a cold and shattering sense of power. I shivered as I lay on the banks and felt that God was grey and cold and violent.

When I finally rose and went inside the house I saw the darkness and comfort no longer as shelter but somehow alien. I felt that the sun was forever in my blood, I was flooded with light, and yet there was the dreadful coldness, as if I would never again belong to the world of the living.

Mother said, 'You had better eat some food. Don't lie in the sun all afternoon. You should rest inside the house.'

We ate our meal in silence. Father never spoke, and while he was gentle with Mother, and always affectionate, he went about his duties as if language had never been made. I think it was because he managed alone the fields, the commerce, the workers. We were too young, and to Mother he never spoke about anything. He ate the food she cooked, and always seemed to delight in it, he said his prayers when all of us gathered in the evenings in a gentle monotone. I think he felt that Grandfather was still there. (I remember waking up one night and seeing Father staring at us as we slept on the mats. In the moonlight his face seemed strange, as if he were trying to possess us, understand us – what he did not dare do when we were awake. When he saw me awake, he turned his head.)

That evening, when we had eaten, Father gave me the Bible to read and what I found was a verse which said, I remember, 'Thou hast known me from my mother's womb.' Perhaps that was when I knew I would serve God and His house. There was a church that was my right to serve, where Grandfather had served. I would go in apprentice to my father's brother who now celebrated the Holy Eucharist there. He was an old man, venerated by all. I was nine years old. I told no one that day, though in some strange way my father understood that I would not after all engage in agriculture. He said it that very day, 'I wanted to begin teaching you the accounts. I think

Behnan can do that when he grows. Learn the psalms well.'

So I was left alone to dream by the side of the river, only appearing at evening to recite a psalm, as the family and servants knelt on the yellow, fraying mats.

When I went to study with Father's brother, Malpan Andreyos, I was thirteen years old. Mother made a white cloak-like dress for me – not quite like a priest's kuppayam or cope but similar enough. She stitched a small round cap of some bright black velvet. It felt warm and snug on my head, it was already a second skin. It was animal-like on my head and when I took it off at night I felt bare and uncomfortable. Mother did not cry, because she said that she had known of this moment from the time of my birth. Father held my hand for a moment – that unaccustomed gesture of affection shook me. His hands were cold, dry, without life almost and we were both embarrassed by my tears which fell on his thin fingers. Behnan was nowhere to be seen, though we heard his voice distantly from the coconut groves. I looked towards the river, as I departed with my maternal uncle. It was a cloudy day, the river looked black and the sugar-cane shivered against the water. The house too closed itself to me, the wooden latticework dropping from the roof like thin creepers were inward looking; the old Persian Cross reflected candlelight bleakly from the door – it was a carving of the cross through which I as a child loved to put my fingers, till one day they got stuck and Mother beat me, while Behnan laughed and stood on his head with delight. The shadows of the mango tree had fallen on the wall, the light was both golden and dull, a storm was on its way.

My mother's brother held my hand, and accompanied me to Malpan's house. This uncle was a tall man, and I found it difficult to walk, chained by his affection. Yet in him I saw both tenderness and authority and I loved him.

'Eat well. Andreyos forgets sometimes when he is at his books.'

'Will you come to see me often?'

'Lukose, you know my work does not allow me much time. I will come after Lent.'

'Will you bring me mangoes from your field?'

'Is that all you want?'

'Bring me a cat too, and mulberries.'

When we reached the Malpan's house it was locked. I looked in through the barred window – the room was dark, musty, there was a table with a clean white cloth on it. After calling 'Andreyos Accha!' several times, my mother's brother Mathappi went to the cottage near the gate. A woman came out, and looked at us for a minute before she went in again. While we waited, a man with a grizzled head and a thin bent body emerged.

'Who is it?'

'I have come with Lukose Achen's grandson.'

'So this is Andreyos Achen's brother's son. How he has grown! Well, Achen is not here. You know me – I look after the graves. You can sit in the church if you like, it is open. Andreyos Achen has gone to a marriage in the next village. He will be back before night.'

Mathappi Achen, as I called him, held my hand and the small bundle of clothes my mother had given me, and we went into the church. The church had been built by my grandfather in 1880; the date was written under the cross above the door. It said 1055. The light had changed again. We sat in the back, on a reed mat, having left our shoes outside. I looked at the altar where I would learn to serve, and felt a deep sense of dread. What mysteries were hidden here? I felt that I would die. The Malpan was a stranger to me – an ascetic, learned old man, saintly almost.

As Mathappi Achen and I sat there the setting sun entered through the western door. The light was everywhere. I could see nothing for the white light. I tried to rise but I was helpless. I prostrated myself forty times, till my knuckles were dark with dust. I knew at the end of it that the lamp hanging from the rafters was lit and that I would one day celebrate the sacrifice, here, in this small lime-washed church.

Mathappi Achen looked at me after my prayers were over and said, 'I have a long journey over the water. My boatman will be impatient. Stay here – you are safe. Andreyos Achen knows you are to join him. I will go now.'

He kissed my brow, and held me by my shoulders. I said nothing.

When Andreyos Achen came back he looked tired and frail. He saw me watching the shadows thrown by the swinging, flickering lamp, touched my shoulder to guide me, saying nothing. I think he too felt that the priestly line would continue, it was necessary at least for Grandfather's sake, but his face was stern, a sense of horror at the closeness he would have to enter into with a young boy.

He showed me to my room in silence. It was very small, having but one window and a narrow bed.

'We will speak tomorrow.'

'I am happy to be with you, Father.'

'We will see. Have you brought your prayer books?'

'I know them by heart.'

'I will hear tomorrow.'

My bed was hard and narrow, but I fell asleep. I woke to the chiming of bells. It was barely dawn. I ran to the river and washed, listening to the birds as they called. When I went inside the small dark house of my uncle the priest, I found there was no food. I longed for the bitter black coffee, tinged with the flavour of wood smoke that my mother made for us. For a moment I thought, 'The old priest hasn't spoken to me, I can still go back.' I saw the little bridge over the Pamba that separated the two hamlets, saw myself running over it, never to return to the church built in 1055 of the Malayalam era. I would marry, Father would build a house for me, I would walk in the rice fields and the slopes of tapioca and pepper that were mine.

Then I smelt the frankincense. It was bitter and fragrant and came to me from the windows of the church. I heard the priest call out 'Kyrie Eleison', Lord have mercy, and I went to join him. He was dressed in robes of gold, his feet shod in red velvet shoes. The church was empty as I kissed the steps and the pillars of the altar. He blessed me with his handcross, and I became like him, a servant, eager to see God, hardly ever succeeding in my desire, yet every day crying out to the people so that by standing at attention they would understand his revelation. At the moment, neither church nor priest, nor the world even, had significance and that was the truth.

river and sea

Leelamma had come with me to the station to meet Job. He was a short thin man, dark, with black large eyes. I recognised him at once from the photographs he had sent me. He dropped his suitcases and with no sign of diffidence he held my hands and said, 'It's you. At last.' I was faintly embarrassed, and tried to pull out of his entrance. Suppressing laughter, Leelamma turned away.

Job was Father's brother. He had been studying architecture in Italy as a young man, when he had met Marcella and married her. Grandfather and Grandmother were upset; there followed the usual tirades and threats of disinheritance, but Job would neither return nor leave the 'Englishkarti' as his mother called Marcella. There were no children, another reason for Grandmother's continuous diatribes.

I was born to Father and Mother when they were very young. Mother had been sixteen and Father barely twenty years old. She was a lovely woman, my mother. I still remember her the day before she died. I was seven years old. Her name was Rahael. We used to live in a large old house. There were wooden walls and ceilings, courtyards, old trees and older furniture. Grandfather, whom we called Appacha, spent most of his time poring over palm-leaf manuscripts with hieroglyphics which he said explained our family genealogy for eighteen generations. His friend Thoma used to laugh at him – 'Why do you need a genealogy? Can't you see your nose?'

Mother tied her hair in a knot and always went barefoot. Her feet were long and once I walked into the room where Father kept his account books. She was sitting on his chair. I couldn't believe it. I was shocked. I had never seen them together alone, Grandmother was always with them. The idea that they slept side by side would have stunned me at that age. I always slept close to Mother. Father slept alone. I had never before seen them together like this. I stared at them, feeling waves of anger and jealousy. They laughed and called out to me, but I ran away to the river. I sat on the steps and I cried till Yohan, my father's elder brother's son, found me and took me to my grandmother. 'Why are you crying?' she asked, holding me against her soft large bosom, where I could see the speck of gold which was her marriage locket.

'Father and Mother are alone together without me.' Grandmother laughed and said, 'I will just call your mother. She has to grate coconuts for dinner.'

The next day my parents went for a wedding in the next village. It was called Mannar, and I'd always loved going there. The school had a heavy bronze bell, and the steps to the church were whitewashed. The river was green, covered with lilac water-hyacinths, and the boats had to fight their way through the root tresses of these water weeds. There was a storm that evening, and my parents never returned. I never saw them again, though they were brought home. I sat on the back steps of the old house and looked deep into the centres of the yellow canna flowers that my father had grown – wanton yellow with red fire lines. I looked inside the flowers for hours till I was dizzy and thought I would fall into their centres and drown.

So I grew up with Grandmother and all my cousins. After my father died, his father put away the lineage story into a shoe box and then took to visiting the river. He would stare at the water, at the strange and shifting reflections. Then he would come home and say nothing. Yohan's father was always having to look after the family business: pepper. I grew up with the raw green beads of pepper, and the rain which fell on the twine and leaves. Yohan's mother was a very gentle woman, but she never had time for me, having seven of her own. Leelamma and Yohan were older than me by five and three years each, but even so, they were my companions. Then when I was eighteen they got married and went to live in their own houses. Leelamma still came to visit us, but these visits were getting more and more infrequent. Her mother-in-law fell ill, there was too much work.

'Leela, you've forgotten me.'

'Anna, how can you say that?'

'Why don't you come home, then?'

'How can I? I'm married now. People will think I'm unhappy if I keep coming home.'

'Are you happy?'

'You've seen Issac. What else could I be?'

'Yohan never comes to see me, now that he's built a house.'

'Why don't you go over, then?'

'Mariam doesn't like me. She leaves me in the outside rooms and goes away.'

'That is right. You hang around Yohan too much. You've both grown up now.'

'But I love him. We've always been friends.'

'He's married now. And he's not your brother. You're his father's brother's daughter. People talk.'

'Won't it ever be the same again?'

'No.'

It was on that day that I wrote to Job, Father's second brother. I sent him an old photograph of Father and Mother and a new one of myself. Twenty-one days later I got a reply. It was on a postcard, and it came from somewhere in Switzerland. He was there on business. Marcella was in Rome where they had a flat. His writing was small and cramped and he closed his letter with the words, 'We have space. Stay with us.'

In my community, those who are far away always return. My grandmother's grief lay in that Job, having married a foreigner, would never come back to her. 'Even if it's only to lie in the mud next to us, it would be enough, but now he'll never come.'

I was surprised by Job's invitation and showed it to Ammachi. She made me explain it to her. Then wiping her eyes with the edge of her gold-embossed shawl, she said, 'Let him come here and take you.'

She seemed to have lost her rancour against Job's attachment to the 'Englishkarti.' She was eighty-five years old now, her eyes blue grey with age. She had never recovered from the loss of my parents, and now that death came close, she wanted me to be settled. For her it seemed perfectly reasonable that Job should come, and that I should be in his care.

'He is busy, and besides he's only asked me for a holiday,' I said, hesitatingly.

'No. Job wants you to live with them.'

It was impossible arguing with Ammachi, so I let it rest. Soon after Job came home.

He was only thirty-seven years old, and looked like Yohan. For the ten days that he stayed in the ancestral house he quarrelled with Ammachi. It was terrible.

'You didn't bring the Madame?'

'Marcella,' Job said softly.

'What kind of name is that? It's not in the Bible.'

'It's a good name.'

'She is not good, I know.'

'You haven't even met her.'

'Cigarettes.'

'She is very gifted. She is well-known in her country. Who cares what you think in this backwater.'

'And her legs. Everyone in the street sees her legs.'

'What about your mother? We all saw her breasts.'

'She had children, she had once provided milk, she was ninety-five. How can there be shame then?'

'My wife is an artist and a good one.'

'Does she bring any money?' Ammachi's eyes were suddenly alert.

'Mother, stop it. I'm going.'

'Take Anna. After I go no one will give her rice.'

'She has her inheritance.'

'And what was it that fed her, clothed her and educated her for all these years?'

'You Nazarenes, you followers of Yeshu Christu, have you never heard of love?'

'What can I do? Abe controls the business. He says there is nothing for her.'

'I'll take her with me.'

Ammachi got up, and held Job's hands and kissed them.

At the end of the month of June – ceaseless rain – Job and I left for Rome. I was so excited, I had dark shadows under my eyes from not sleeping for almost ten days. The whole village turned out to see us go, and anxious faces peered in at us when the taxi's wheels churned in the deep sea sand. The river is on the east, the sea is close by, on the other side.

Father George, my teacher, looked in through the glass. He was desperately trying to say something.

'Don't forget your prayers, Anna,' I finally heard, as I lowered the pane.

'No, I won't forget.'

'Don't forget your Malayalam. Have you taken the Gundert?'

Job asked, turning back to look at me, 'What on earth

is the Gundert? And I must buy you a box. You have a tin trunk? I didn't even know they still existed.'

'It's a dictionary. The Gundert is an English–Malayalam dictionary. Father George is afraid I'll forget to read and write the mother tongue.'

'Write every week. Don't forget the algebra,' the old man shouted once more.

'Yes, Father.'

'Meet Father Agnello. A Catholic, but a good man. Holy.'

It started to rain. I saw Yohan. He was looking at Mariam and smiling. He looked towards me and waved. The taxi began to move, and then through a blur of tears, I saw Yohan open out a large black umbrella and Mariam stood close against him.

Marcella was wonderful. She was older than Job, and the love between them was so tangible I was forever surprised by it. Job stopped speaking Malayalam to me, and I was forced to learn Italian. My English was very good, because Father George had a degree in literature, in philosophy and in theology from Cambridge. He had been our parish priest for twenty years – unusual for our sect where priests were constantly transferred. It was he who had educated me, and by the time I was sixteen I had read almost everything that he had. The Russians were indecipherable to me, and Father said that I would have to wait till I was thirty before I could begin. I sometimes told Yohan what I read and he would look strangely at me. His eyes were narrow and black, and his cheekbones so sharp that they jutted through his skin.

'You don't even know how to cook.'

'Shall I translate Aristotle's *Politics* for you?'

'That's all very well. You had better marry soon, Anna. You have charm, but no beauty. Your father died too early. You can't even cook or sew. You're thin like your mother – she almost died when she gave birth to you.'

'Yohan, why are you saying all this?'

'I'm worried about you. And you should stop coming to see me. I'll talk to Father about finding a match for you.'

How long ago all that seemed here in Rome. I realised as the years passed that love threatened us both. I understood, sitting under another kind of sun, why Yohan no longer acknowledged me.

Marcella never talked to me of marriage. She bought me an expensive camera almost as soon as I arrived.

'We can't afford to send you to the University. We want you to have the best, but university – no. We cannot afford. You're too late to sculpt. The camera is good, you learn and sell. That is how you will live.'

So my future was carved out, and I spent those early months walking miles every day, in the cold breeze and the spring rain, learning to use a camera. My early photographs – now with Father George – were mainly of fountains and plazas, colonnades and arches. Marcella was not pleased.

'Stupid tourist bitch,' I heard her screaming to Job.

'Marcella, she's a child, from the country. Don't speak like that.'

'Let her hear what I think.'

Two years later I did a study of the Colosseum. The

earth was deeply stenched with rain, weeds grew. I sent
them to a German magazine which printed them at once.
Celebration! Marcella was pleased at last. She gave me
one of her odd, rare and brilliant smiles.

I wanted to go back home, but Job dissuaded me.

'Things will not be the same. Ammachi is dead, what is
there to go for?'

'Yohan is there, and Leelamma.'

'Yohan? That silent boy, Abe's son? You want to see
him?'

'I want to hear the rain, I want to eat mangoes, sit by
the river.'

'You're a fool. Nothing is the same ever. Ask Marcella
for money if you want to go. I have none now.'

So I never went back. Sometimes in the dark green
Roman street, ancient cobbles under my feet. I would
think of the old house where I grew up. There were children, frogs, spiders, crows in the backyard, dark recesses,
mangoes ripening in hay, and hens laying eggs in a chest
of rice. I missed the high pitched Syrian chants from the
village church, and the white cotton clothes edged with
gold metallic thread that our women wore. One day I
would go back to my ancient village where the wind
brought to us the sound of the sea, and the hush of river
water.

waiting

It was the dry bare-bones of a long summer. I walked in the dust, with the hot winds blowing around me, paper scrapping in the alleys, the city deserted in the glare of the afternoon sun. I walked to the old fort. It was green and cool, the grass growing wild, the moat a little murky, but glistening silver where it escaped the shadows of old mortar. I heard the strange guttural calls of water birds, and the summer became at once another. I was seventeen then. The memory became an incandescent bubble in which I lay, slothful.

I don't know how long I had been lying in the shadows of the old peepal. Vulture droppings had made the tree alien, and I sensed the death in the old tree – its gnarled roots were exposed like the knees of crones, and its scabby trunk veered upward. A million tiny ants crawled out of a hole and marched in single file around and around its base.

I knew it was madness to stay, but the tentacles of time caught me – the fort so old and unknown, spoke to me in a hundred ways. It was dusk when I arose and saw to my surprise that I was not alone. The man was tall, with the narrow brown eyes that I had known once before, both laughter and arrogance in them. He was older by twenty years, and I felt a deep sense of dread.

'So you still come here.'

'Yes, sometimes – when it gets too hot.'

He pointed at the steps where we had sat, those long years ago in our childhood.

'Do you remember the flies? They used to circle us,' he said.

'Kings and horses, I remember, but not the flies,' I laughed, looking at him, forgetting the years in between.

We had sat on the steps many times with our hands locked together, afraid to make love because I was too young to ask, and he, old-fashioned, knew we were not destined to marry. I remembered the dreadful intensity of our eyes as they looked into each others', the world sailing past, and yet beyond it – a laughter which would redeem us, would allow us to jump down and go walking barefoot over the ancient graves and the jagged ends of broken walls.

'Why did you go away like that?' I asked him.

'You were too young for me. You understood nothing about me.'

'Are you married now?'

He took out a smooth black wallet, and from it pictures of his large, lovely wife and his perfect children. They were American, all of them. So was he, down to his Reebok shoes and his wine-coloured tie.

'I missed you,' I said.

'You should have written.'

'You left no address.'

He held my hands again.

'Give me a hug.'

It was so American, so casual and innocent, that I had to hold him. His body felt the same, but it was softer, older – a body which did not have the tautness of desire, but had known love and the gentleness of wife and children, safe house, a big golden dog to walk to the woods.

We disentangled, and he smiled at me. It began to rain, and we went our different ways without looking back. It was too late to ask him 'What did you do?' Nor did he question me: 'What have you become?' or 'Do you still live in the same house?' Perhaps it was because we understood that our worlds could not meet, that in our tenuous and placid worlds the other was only a shadow.

My work on Carson McCullers had come to a standstill. I had no way of deciphering the silences in the narratives. McCullers had lived the world I had known and felt as a child.

I had read her short stories over and over again, and all the poignancy of childhood, of unutterable desires, of loneliness and of wanting, came back to me. I had a McCullers complex, and it ran deep. I applied for a grant and went to a university town in America. No, I told myself, it's not in the hope of seeing Karan again, it's just a coincidence that I know he lives there too.

The city I lived in during that summer was large and open and cold. Brownstone buildings, no trees. Billboards. Greek cafes. Bookshops and an aquarium, with an eleven-dollar entrance fee where I would go when I was lonely to look at the fish, and be crushed in the whirlpool of people. It saved me from the alienation of the neutral city. Americans had children. I realised this when I went to the aquarium. I suppose, in my heart, I hoped that I would meet my childhood friend again, his beautiful wife with the yellow hair and the children who looked like his mother from Jullundar. Where else, living in a city which didn't really respect children, would he take them?

Then one day, I saw them. It was exactly as I had imagined. He was carrying his daughter aloft on his shoulder, safe from the crowds; his wife and son were behind, carrying bags of popcorn and wild-coloured umbrellas. It was raining outside, their hair was shining with rain drops in the blue dark, the artificial underwater world of the aquarium.

'Karan!' I said, 'Do you remember me?' I was good at subterfuge.

'Elizabeth! Of course, meet my wife Gina, and these are my kids. What brings you here? Where are you staying?'

'At the University.'

'Here? You're on a trip?'

'I live here.'

His wife looked at me, and smiled, and held my hands, and said, 'You must come for lunch on Sunday. It's not often that Karan meets friends from India.'

'I'd love to, but I'm leaving for home tomorrow, for Kerala. You remember my home country, Karan.'

'Yes, I took Gina there soon after we were married – boat rides across the backwater and all that. But then it rained – like mad – and we could find nothing that she could eat except bananas. It's wild rain forest, your homeland. I never imagined. I couldn't cope with those spiders though. You're leaving tomorrow? That's a pity. We must keep in touch.'

He gave me his glossy visiting card, and his children, standing there, smiled and smiled at me, while his wife chattered about English studies and India. Neither of them had heard of McCullers and thought her a man. We walked together around the glass cases of the aquarium where large and well fed sharks swam in circles and in boredom, looking at us with dull-mirror eyes, wishing they were hungry and the sea was open.

Karan and I looked at each other when one circle around the alive and entombed fish was done, and the floodgates of memory opened again. The crowds separated us from his family.

'You still love me, don't you? I should have waited.'

'I'm leaving tomorrow,' I said, wiping my tears, carefully, in case the colours smudged.

'You're not. You always were a terrible liar. You came here looking for me. This is your idea of revenge. Well, this time, it's goodbye,' and he strode away back to the waiting half circle on the other side of the exhibits.

It was raining again, as my taxi left the city down the dark and gleaming roads. I would be back in the Fall, I had a teaching fellowship in New York, but meanwhile I would accept Benjamin's offer of marriage. I would go back to the old cardamom estate, and to my father's brother who would ask for Benjamin on my family's behalf, for me. Ben had waited too long.

*　　*　　*

Benjamin's estate was next to ours, and our families had always planned that we should marry. He had waited for me – waited and waited, I should say – but I was so hopelessly in love with Karan that it seemed that I would never come out of it. But now I had. I felt I had. When I told my Uncle that I was ready to marry, he laughed and said, 'You're thirty. Who shall I ask?'

'Benjamin,' I said.

'Benjamin? But he was married last summer when you went to America. Why did you go? He asked you to stay.'

'Oh hell,' I said, involuntarily. We don't speak like that in front of our uncles.

'Don't be silly, Eli. You shouldn't talk like that. We'll find someone else. Lucky that you have property or else it would have been impossible, even if you were ten years younger which you're not. We'll find a boy who is already in the States or in the Gulf. I'll talk to the broker.'

'The broker?'

'Yes, you just pay him a commission on the dowry you plan to give at betrothal. How much are you going to give – rather, what shall we say we are giving?'

'Uncle, I'm going back to Delhi today. I don't think I'll marry this summer.'

'You really are insane. I told my brother not to over-educate you. Just look at you. Dressed like a man. Pants. Even a belt. And your buttocks showing. Can't you pull out your shirt at least. And lipstick. Someone will think you've gone mad. Well, go see your grandmother. She's been waiting to see you. I can't drive you out to the airport today. I have work on the plantation. You go tomorrow.'

Uncle was furious. He looked at me through narrow, cynical eyes, denigrated everything I was or had done. I fled to the small dark room with its low entrance, where Grandmother lay resting. It was a pretty room, though so shadowed I could hardly see her. The smell of paddy boiling in large urns came wafting in from outside. There were small square windows with delicate white cotton drapes. I could see the workers threshing the grain. Her bed was narrow, but made of dark glossy redwood with elaborate canework at the head where she was propped up reading her Bible. I sat on the bench near the window waiting for her to look up.

'And Jesus wept,' she said, ending the lesson.

'Hello, Ammachi.'

'Eli, so you've come. Not even a postcard. Benjamin wanted to invite you for his marriage, but we didn't even have your address. How can you disappear like that?'

'I left the address with Uncle,' I said, smiling at her. Her collarbones stood out sharp and clear from the edges of the large clean white blouse she always wore.

'He said he didn't have it. The important thing is, you didn't write. What have you been doing? Look at your hair. Like a hen's tail. And no earrings. People in America seem as badly attired as people in Delhi. Have you eaten? We've made three kinds of fish for you. It's so wonderful you've come back. We must find a boy for you . . . Your father's left you enough money, thank God!'

'I'm leaving tomorrow. I have to get some books from the house in Delhi, and then I'll go back to America.'

'You're leaving tomorrow? But you've just arrived. You always lacked common sense. That's why it's so difficult to get you married off. Benjy was such a good man. He would have looked after you well. But what's the use. A boy needs someone who can cook and clean, not someone who reads all the time.'

'I'm thirty, I don't need a boy. I have to go. I must go. I find the rain oppressive. My books are already damp, by tomorrow the gum holding them will have gone completely.' I was almost weeping.

'Rain, oppressive? But without rain things don't grow. It's true that there is no fish, in the rains the fish just disappear. Where do all the fish in the sea go? Ouseph says that it's dangerous to fish. I've never been near the sea, so I won't know. Eli, we were lucky today. We made three kinds of fish for you. Go and eat, you're tired.'

'I hate fish,' I said stonily.

'You're just like your father. He was my favourite. Your uncle is not at all like him. I really had to talk your grandfather into giving your father that chunk of property. Your uncle is still mad with me. And your grandfather kept saying, "But he's a teacher. What'll he do with money? He doesn't know how to invest." Anyway, you're taken care of. But one thing, Eli, if another year goes by, no one will marry you. Oil your hair at least, it's gone copper.'

'I don't want to marry, I want to study.'

'But you're thirty. How can you keep studying? Anyway, go and eat. I'm tired.'

She put her beautiful silver head on the pillow, and her creased soft face looked tired.

'Come and see me before you go. I'll give you a bottle of Kashayam. It's made of gooseberries I cured ten years ago. It will make your blood flow.'

'I wouldn't touch it. The last concoction you gave me made my head swim.' I bent to kiss her.

'Thin-blooded, that's why,' she said, blessing me, with her dry papery old hands on my head and my cheeks.

I went out into the bright monsoon sunlight. After the rain, because the atmosphere is clean, the light is always strong.

Centipedes crawled out from beneath stones and locked in coitus. They looked like they would multiply at great speed and take over the land.

I looked at my thin flat stomach covered by my olive shirt. Would I have children? Was it important? Would I love a man again, and keep a house, and forget the eternity of waiting that I had just passed? I went in to eat my three kinds of fish for lunch.

summer, and then the rain

The mango trees were in bloom as he came home that summer. They splayed out over the roof of the house, and he knew that later, as it grew hotter, the fruit would hang green and heavy, and then become golden in the chests of dark teakwood.

His sister opened the door. When he looked at her he knew that the summers had passed without their knowing. His first remembrances were of her as a child – thin, with slanting black eyes, like all the women in his father's family: the many aunts who had dominated his childhood. Her face had a strange beauty, translucent almost, but she did not smile at him.

'What's happened to you,' she said. 'You look sick.'

'Came home to die, didn't I tell you that. You never reply to any of my letters.'

She said nothing but took him into the large dark rooms of their ancient home. The taravat, as his mother called it, always reminded him of the long Biblical genealogies his father had made him read by candlelight. How tedious it had seemed, this preoccupation with ancestry, with sonhood, with naming. He was glad he had no property to

congeal in inheritance, no child to take over the preoccupation of being an 'old line'. Under this roof Ivan begat
Yohan and Yohan begat John, and John begat Yohan and
Yohan begat Yohanan, century after century with deliber-
ate certainty. He thought of his sister, and the silence that
followed her birth. At that very moment, when no bells
clanged, and no sweets were made with jaggery and rice,
he had resolved to end this torment of patrilineality once
and for all. He would not marry.

At work his friends used to ask him, 'How can you have
such a name, "Ivan"?'

'Ivan is my father's name, Malayalam for John – may be
Syrian, or Greek, who knows? – our ancestors were bap-
tised by St Thomas, the disciple of Christ, and so we have
the names of Jesus' friends and followers.'

'What is the unpronounceable name you hide in the
initial V?'

He would say, 'Vazhayil – the name of our house,' and
his terseness always surprised them.

He never wanted to share Vazhayil with anyone. The
dark cool interiors filled often enough the labyrinths of
his own memory. He remembered, too, with a certain
detachment his father's hands with their three fingers
missing – chopped off by a neighbour's kitchen knife
in a mango orchard. The neighbour was his father's
brother's son, Thoma. They still talked to one another,
now that his father was dead, and curiously Ivan bore no
grudge.

He put his bags on the bed, and listened for a moment
to the creaking – a circular creaking – and asked what it
was.

'It's the fan,' said his sister from the kitchen. 'Don't you remember? Father had it put in in 1937.'

He looked up and saw it dangerously veering in a circular motion. Its flat blades were painted cream and black wires threaded across a wooden ceiling. A naked light bulb hung dangerously close, swinging in vicarious motion. Outside the crows were calling out near the kitchen. It was still morning.

'How was the journey?'

'It was hot, but it rained once. I couldn't eat anything.'

At the table, as she put out the food for him, he looked at her closely. Her face was deeply lined, and on her hands the veins stood out, deep and thick and blue, like the outlines of bare trees. She poured out his tea. Why was it so thick, he wondered, like some viscous soup.

'I made it just the way you like it,' she said, stirring the tea leaves continuously.

He did not reply.

'It's Lent, isn't it?' he said, looking at what she had cooked, for there was no meat or fish.

'For me, it's always Lent.'

'Oh God, no.'

'I'll cook for you if you like, but you will have to pay. You know my finances, I can hardly manage.'

'Is that why you don't eat, then?'

'No, I like to keep the fasts. Now for me, every day is holy and every day I take the Eucharist.'

'You must be the only one in the village then.'

'The churches are always crowded. You left the faith. Joined the Communists? Father said you even had a membership card. Here things are the same. It's you who changed . . . Eat now, I will ask Pappenchettan to buy fish from tomorrow.'

'I can't eat much, but it's something I remember of our childhood. With tamarind?'

'Yes.'

He slept the whole afternoon, and is body rested against the golden reed mat preserved from his mother's time. The edges were frayed, but the softness was wonderful. He felt as if he were sleeping on fresh-smelling hay, and when he awoke it was dark and raining outside. Annama had lit the lamps, for the lights had gone, snapped by the storm. The fat brown beetles he remembered from his childhood were buzzing around the flames.

He went out onto the porch. His feet were bare and he could feel the gravel brought in from some ancient riverbed. Each stone was small and round, smooth, and yet harsh at the same time under his feet.

He walked down to the canal where the tributaries of rivers moved around the town like silver coiled snakes.

The lights of the street shone on the water and he stopped to light a beedi.

'Ah! Ivan, is it you?' It was his cousin.

'Yes, I came this morning. How is Eliyamma?'

'In good health. Let us walk together. I heard you were sick. Cancer. Is it true? You look much the same.'

'Three months, they said.'

'Well, we all have to go. When they put the earth on you, how will you care?'

'Is there any room in the cemetery? I heard you could not buy land anymore.'

'Oh, be buried with your father.'

'No, we never got on. You know I hated him.'

'That's why you still talk to me. Those three fingers I took off him. I still dream about it. They lay in the corner of the field for quite some time. And it was all about a square of land smaller than a kerchief.'

'Don't think about it.'

'Will I see you in church tomorrow?'

'No, I hate the old priest. Why can't he throw off his long beard, those black robes. Is he closer to Christ because of them?'

'Still the same Ivan. Drink from the holy cup. Your disease will go.'

'My father drank from it every Sunday and his fingers never grew.'

'All right then. Tell Annama that I will send the man to fell the coconuts tomorrow.'

Ivan watched Thomas as he moved away into the darkness of the narrow lane. He was still burly at sixty-five, his legs showed the clear blue network of veins as he strode with his *mundu* hitched above his knees. His teeth, though betel-stained, were strong. There was something coarse about him, a little brutal, and yet his features, typical of all of them – hooked nose and broad brow – still had the old grace. Thoma had wanted to marry Ivan's sister, but the old man their father, had thrashed him with a walking stick. Thoma was seventeen years old then – not likely to forget that thrashing.

Annama had told Ivan about it, many years later. She too had not married. Their father had died, and their mother wanted Anna at home with her. Ivan had tried to persuade Anna that she should allow him to arrange a marriage for her – some widower perhaps who would not object to her age. It was then that she told him the story of Father's anger.

'He shouted all day and all night. He ate nothing. He flung food off the table. Poured buckets of water on our beds so that we could not sleep. He would say again and again, 'Filthy, filthy! Seven generations must pass before blood can be shared again. If he looks at you once more. I will finish him.' I can't forget Father saying all this. It was a sin to love Thoma. I could not commit it. But I cannot marry anyone, then.'

So the thrashing had taken place, and its retaliation. Annama never spoke to Thoma, but nevertheless he showed his love in many small ways. She never refused him, but it was understood that Jesus would judge them, and the silence between them was understood by their larger family. Ivan was sick of all that.

He would bang his fists on the table and shout.

'Not Jesus. What do you mean, "Jesus is coming". It's the bomb . . . the bomb will come.'

'Jesus *will* come. It says so in Revelation. Your Bible is still here. I'll get it for you.'

He could see his Bible, childhood's text – yellow, paper crackling, backbone frayed, faded leaves and flowers of a long gone summer still keeping place.

'Annama, the disease will wipe me out, the bomb will wipe out the earth. Where is Jesus in all this? I've got a translation of Orwell's *1984*. Here, take it.'

'Jesus will be there. I believe. The sheep will be separated from the goats.'

'You be the sheep and I the goat?'

'No, Ivan, you are a good man. You will not be sent away.'

'Don't forget, I want the cheapest coffin, and no lining. Mango wood will do, and no cross.'

'Ivan, you will go as befits the status of Kochumathu's son.'

There was no arguing with her. He would get up from the table. The pain beginning to sear him again had become a blinding preoccupation, an obsession, a desire for calm that would never be satisfied. In some strange way all that remained of his days in this old house in the ancestors' village, were the memories of childhood overlapping with the pain that engulfed everything.

When the end came it was early in the morning. He saw the sun rise, and felt the air cool on his body. The trees were dark and soft with rain. The earth would be wet. He had a sudden longing to walk barefoot to the canal, and to look into the water for one last time. He heard Annama moving around – shuddering into wakefulness. He saw the purple orchids, the large white spider lilies, heard the fluttering of pigeons. And that was all.

something barely remembered

When Chako came to live in a small village in the hills of North Malabar, the people took to him at once. He was a tall man, thin, a little stooped, and his beard was so long it touched his chest. That was unusual in that area, where men were clean shaven. He found a place to stay in a household which consisted of a man called George, and his little daughter Anna. Chedathi, an old woman living in the outskirts of the village, could come to cook for them and wash clothes. The house was never dusted; it was always dark, littered with clothes, Anna's books and papers, many stray cats and George Saar's leather-covered account books. Strangely enough, there were no flies.

George Saar had never known Chako before, but while climbing down the slope from the church, where he spent every evening doing the accounts, he heard a slither behind him. Chako in his clean white mundu, hitched above his knees, umbrella under his arm, had slipped over some red gravel.

'What is it, missed your step?'

'I come from the paddy lands. Not used to this.'

'Who do you want to meet?'

'I'm a doctor, a green herbs man.'

'You won't get any custom here. Everyone makes their own medicines.'

'No, no, I have come to collect them.'

'Don't you leave that to your assistants?'

'I'm writing a book. Everyone in the West wants our knowledge, we must share our ancient texts. I've come to draw pictures of the plants, and then if I find a nice place to stay, I'll do the writing here as well.'

George Saar took him to his house, and then almost at once asked Chako if he would like to live with them. Chako looked at the man. He had a strangely effeminate face, eyes very large and melancholic and a blue haze on his morning-razored face. It was a face that seemed to float in water, drowning in some unformed and congealing grief.

Chako said he would pay him two hundred rupees a month, which George Saar refused. He said, 'It's enough that you are a man of knowledge. And widely travelled. Not many people in our village can speak English, and we need some correspondence handled in a court case against a chemical company. A proper doctor is always useful. Which church do you belong to?'

'Anglican.'

'No harm in that, you can come to worship with us. We are Mar Thoma. The subscription is thirty rupees a year, and I'll take that from you now.'

While George Saar took out the little yellow receipt, Chako looked around the house. He would have preferred to stay in a larger house, perhaps by himself. But then, for a start this would do. He put his small blue canvas bag on the bed, and was removing his broad-strapped Bata shoes when a cat suddenly jumped on his shoulder. It had been sitting unnoticed on the mosquito-net bar over the bed, and while it startled him, he was not averse to cats and put it gently down.

There was a small window at the side of the bed. The wall was made of thick brown teak wood, and from the window he could see acres of green banana trees. The leaves were thick, green, mottled with yellow in places, and the maroon cone flowers with their ivory nectar thick stalks pushed out from every one. It would be a good crop. A child's head appeared at the window – an untidy child, but a pretty one. He noticed she was wearing red beads around her neck, and that her hair was cut very short. The long skirt did not match the blouse, for both were made from different cloths, different textures by perhaps different tailors.

'What's your name?'

'Anna. Why are you sitting on my bed?'

'I thought it was mine.'

'Achennae! Achennae!'

The child ran screaming for her father.

He met her again at dinner time. George Saar, it seemed for all his penury, had one weakness, which was for candles. He had lit six, where two would have done. They made a bright warm glow, penumbras merging into each other. The child ate well, though a cat sat on her lap and made small quick movements with its paws every time she picked the fish on her plate. Sometimes she would look at Chako, and there was a strange darting awareness when she did that. He was surprised, because he was forty years old, and though he knew he was attractive to women, he had not expected a child to express these shadows of desire.

At night, as he slept near the window on the other side of the house, which overlooked a small rounded hill beyond which there was a narrow stream, he saw in a dream Anna and George. They had encircled him with bamboos, which were bare of leaves. They would not let him leave. He turned then before his eyes, into a magnificent golden snake – large, convoluted, flecked, yellow and tame. He woke to a sense of shame, the room in which he lay dark and heavy, the night sealing him in.

Anna brought him his coffee in the morning. They had a cow, it seemed, for the milk was thick and smelt of grass, insects, and he could almost see the softly ruminating cow. The fireflies, which at night had encrusted the wall and the windows, were now pale green worms. Looking at Anna he remembered the dream. With a child's licence she got into his bed and put her arms around him, nuzzling his beard. He was frightened, repelled, and he pushed her.

'I must start the day. Haven't you got school?'

'No, it's the holidays. Can't I come with you?'

'Where?'

'Father said you were going to look for herbs. I'll show you where they grow.'

'All right. I'll be ready in an hour.'

When she had gone, he took a switch of palm leaves and swept out his room. He straightened the worn grey sheet on the bed, and hung his coloured sarong which he had slept in on a plastic rope above the bed. He washed on the verandah outside his room, where bronze vessels were kept filled with water. There were ants and small leaves floating in them, but it felt chill and clean.

'Mother committed suicide you know. She hanged herself in the back room where you are sleeping.'

Annama was holding his hand as they walked through the dark glades of rubber. Blue birds flew toward the water. There was something strange about the light, a little ominous, an alienness – the trees rising into the sky, tall, gaunt, their leaves thick and almost black-green. Chako didn't know what to say to the child.

'She was only twenty, you know.'

'How old were you?'

'I don't know. Chedathi told me about her. I never saw her. But people always say that she was only twenty. Father has a picture of her. It's in his box. I'll show it to you when we go home.'

'I don't think I should see it, Anna. After all, if it's in his box, it's because he doesn't want everyone to see it.'

'You won't go away, will you, because I told you?'

'I'm only here for this one day, Anna. In the evening I must catch the bus to Trivandrum.'

'Chakocha, don't go. Father said you would live with us. Father doesn't love me. Please stay with us. What I said about Mother wasn't true. She was ill, and she died when I was born, in a hospital. I promise you, she didn't hang herself. I just said that to make you feel sorry for me.'

'I'm sorry for you anyway, Anna. You'll be all right. Now let's look for these plants.'

She ran a little to keep up with him, and when they

came out of the rubber lands, it was a relief. The sun was shining, he could see the soft outlines of the herbs that he sought. He knelt down there, and began to uproot them, carefully placing them in the large file he had brought. They were healthy specimens, and he wished that he had not met George or Anna, and had found a more impersonal residence for himself. He had met the Councillor, the Development Officer, a lawyer and several merchants the previous day – and all of them had been very courteous. He could have spent a month in Puthen-kavu, and no one would have been disturbed by his presence, nor he by theirs. Already because of that chance encounter with George he was trapped in some kind of unhealthy situation. When he looked for Anna an hour later he could not see her.

'Anna, Anna?'

'Chakochaya, here I am.'

He looked up, and found her directly above him in the fork of a large mango tree. She had been watching him all the time, and her face looked small and tense.

'Come down, I want to go to the other side of the river.'

'I shan't come down unless you promise you will live with us.'

'Don't be foolish. I have an old mother I have to return to.'

'I'll not come down then.'

'Do what you like.'

He began to stride away – feeling helpless and angry. He walked till the edge of the river, and then called out to her again. She did not answer, but kept looking at him, her eyes small and angry.

'I'll tell your father.'

'He's at the Loan Office.'

'I'm going then.'

'If I fall down, I'll break my bones and no one will find me.'

'All right, I'll stay.'

She scrambled down. She was laughing, a child again with no remembrance of power.

'I'll call the boatman. You stay here,' she said.

Chako wandered into the water. A small brown snake crept out from behind a rock, and he stepped back quickly.

Anna came back with the boatman. He had a long pole with him, and his bare torso gleamed and glistened in the sunlight with oil and sweat. He was a short fellow, wearing a small rough towel, and although not more than thirty, his teeth were like scraps of betelnut.

'Where does Saar want to go?'

'The other side.'

'Why not cross at the bridge?'

'Where is it?'

'A kilometre from here. If you come with me, it will cost you two rupees to cross.'

'That's all right.'

'Let's go then. Leave the child here. The river is deep and the boat won't take three.'

'All right.'

Anna watched as Chako got into the boat. It swayed, as it tried to free itself from the tethering rope, and he almost lost his footing. She would have laughed, he knew, so he did not look at her. He wondered for a moment whether he could not just leave when he got to the other side. The loss of his bag and the few things he had brought with him would not mean much.

Kuttan untied the rope, and got in with him. It was a canoe, and it rocked violently again. There was no place to sit, and Chako stood uncertainly in the middle. Kuttan used his pole to punt, his body heaving as he pushed into the deep black mud of the river. Anna looked far away, and already Chako felt relieved, a passing stranger.

'Poor child, she doesn't have a mother.'

'She does have a mother, except that she is a whore.'

'I thought she was dead.'

'Dead to the people in this village maybe. She lives in Bombay. She ran off with a rich man, he spoke another language and drove a car.'

'How did he get here?'

'He came here – in a car, you know – came to see this place. What there is to see I don't know. His wife – the one he was married to – collected old boxes it seems. You know the ones our grandmother used to keep their clothes in. Strange, when we no longer have use for things, someone else wants them. You are here to collect green medicines, I heard.'

They had reached the other shore. Chako was burning under the heat of the sun. He wished he had carried his umbrella with him. Kuttan helped Chako out, and then having taken his money strode off toward the cool thatched eaves of the toddy shop.

That afternoon as he had his lunch in a canteen where the buttermilk slopped over the rim of white ceramic jars he heard that a child had been found drowned in the river at Puthenkavu. He wondered for one horrible terrified moment if it was Anna, but he never went back. His belongings, without the blue bag they had been in, arrived by post a year afterwards at his mother's house. They were stitched up in an old pillow cover, but there was no note inside.

It was twelve or fifteen years later that Chako met a woman at a party in Zurich. It was one of those occasions when white wine was drunk in great quantities, and the lake was somnolent and black, a kind of rippled glass.

There were anthropologists and faith healers and medical practitioners. Chako noticed the woman at once, knew that she would be called Sarah or Mariam or Anna, maybe Sosha (for Susan). She had smooth black hair and almond-shaped eyes, reminiscent of sea journeys over the Arabian Sea to Malabar, and the pallor of skin that sheltered women have. She was with a very large man, an ox of a man, a water diviner. When Chako stood near him the water diviner trembled and heaved and almost rotated on some internal axes.

'Aquatic Astral Sign? Pisces?' he said, and Chako nodded, surprised.

Chako watched the woman for a while – there was something about her face, her eyes, the way she looked and murmured which reminded him of a child briefly met.

People were still talking about the evening seminar, and there was no sense of the day having broken into its compartment of leisure time.

'The paper on health and astrology was bizarre.'

'Interesting though that Sylvia Plath's mother was a Paracelsus scholar.'

'Who?'

'Plath.'

'What did she do?'

'Wrote poetry.'

'Must be, everyone writes poetry in this field.'

Chako moved away before he could be drawn into conversation with people who barely knew one another, but acted for five days as if they were intimates. He had already been by the lake, to the woods near the zoo where he heard the mournful calling of elephants dreaming of swamps by teak forests. He had even been to some of the churches, where the bells rang but no one went unless it was to a Bach recital. It was a banker's town. He liked Sumkatra Street best with its large shops full of carpets and masks and incense. He felt comforted there, at sights of the 'exotic east'. The masks grimaced back at him, reminding him of home, and the emotional intensity of life, for here in Zurich, the faces were as finely tailored as costumes.

The woman he had been looking at came towards him. He was right, she was from back home. Sosha.

'I heard you yesterday. You were very good,' she said, tinkling the ice about in the amber glass. Her jewels were perfectly matched, and she wore indigo.

'It's fifteen years since I began this work. I feel far removed from what I am saying or doing. It's much more exciting to be thinking it out.'

'Where did you collect your data?'

'In a village called Puthenkavu.'

Shadows crossed her face. Her eyes became narrow and withdrew into some menacing inner space.

'How odd. I once lived there.'

'You. When was this.'

'Twenty years ago? I was twenty then.'

'You father's name?'

'They called him Ivanios. But he was from another village called Tenapally. I lived at Puthenkavu because I was married there.'

'But your husband – Azor, I met him yesterday at lunch – he's not from home.'

'No. We must talk sometime. Tomorrow I'm planning to look at the University and the old quarters. Would you be free?'

'Yes, certainly. Where shall we meet?'

'At the meeting of Weinberg Street and St Moritz Street.'

'I don't know them.'

'Below the clock at the Autobahnof?'

'I'll be there at eleven.'

She went away without saying any more. Chako felt irritable at having his precious day taken away from him. But it was an odd coincidence and he knew he was entangled.

The next morning he had croissants which his tongue could not pronounce, try as he would. So he asked for 'round bread' and orange juice. There was a delicate old woman, in a rose pink blouse and a tight black skirt – eighty if anything, but with purple eyeshadow and scarlet lipstick – who sat across him and questioned him about India.

'Your people are very brilliant. It is I'm sure because

they eat hot curry powder every day. I once tried it. I bought curry powder, mixed a spoon in a glass of water and drank it. I never tried again.'

He looked at her disbelievingly. She spent the whole hour chatting about the cigarette company she owned at Baar.

'My father wanted a son. I had to become his son. I never married. I took over the company. I come to the Astor for breakfast so that I can see people. It's lonely in my flat. I must visit your country one day. Perhaps in my next life – karma you say – I shall marry and have children. To bear a child must be a miracle.'

When Chako left the room he felt heady with vicariously inhaled cigarette smoke, and laughter, for the old woman had so much courage and guile.

It was cold outside. He looked with wonder at the large imprints which he left behind in the dirty, half melted snow. 'I passed this way though I might never breathe this air again, or see the white mountain flowers growing delicately against a city wall.' He felt strangely happy, a spider who had not yet spun a web, aloof, astray, looking for crevice and shaft as if they were his to know. Boys sped past him on roller skates, and the tang of orange juice was still on his tongue. He saw Sosha waiting at the kiosk outside the station. She was wearing boots and jeans and an army jacket.

'Sosha.'

'Shoshanna really, but my husband calls me Sasha.'

'It suits you.'

'Shall we walk? I must talk to you. When you spoke about Puthenkavu, I was startled, shocked.'

She stopped to drink water at a fountain. Jets of cold clear water spilled out of a medieval lion's mouth. The wind blew cold, and the early geraniums were out on the window boxes. There was no washing hanging out, and no sunshine – only a clear grey day. The hoardings were fluorescent, about the only colour that he could see other than the white of the houses and the green of trees. Chako drank at the rim of the fountain, and was startled at the effervescence of the water as it spilled down his throat.

'I wondered if you had met my husband.'

'There was a child?'

'Yes, a daughter. I abandoned her when she was three months old.'

'Why?' He took out his handkerchief, washed the night before with a minuscule square of hotel soap. He looked carefully at the frayed edges. Sea tides of fear threatened to swallow him. She didn't look at him.

'I was twenty. I met Azor when he came to our house looking for antiques. I fell in love with him. It was pretty wordless really. I mean, we shared nothing – neither past, nor a culture, nor a single idea. It was silent and engulfing, like a seed in the earth, like a bookmark keeping a place, like unknown streams in some strange valley. Nothing seemed important to me then other than persuading him to take me away. He was seventeen years older than me, married with a child. You can't imagine how terrible it all was. And yet, I knew what I was doing. I felt sorry for George, and for the little baby. But then I would think that the baby was better off with George's mother, in fact, in those early weeks it was she who took care of the child. I didn't even know how to hold her. Mothering isn't instinctual, is it? I mean it's got to be learnt. I never gave myself the chance. She must be grown now. I wonder how she looks. Azor would not let me have any children. He said that if I had abandoned a child once, I could do it again. He bore tremendous guilt about his own family and what he had done by leaving them.'

They walked under the bridge by the river, and watched an old man and his wife feeding the ducks. The shadows of the trees lay across the water in orderly rows. The shops were all closed – it was a long weekend and Zurich had emptied itself out as people went to the resort towns. The streets belonged to the foreign tourist, camera in hand, calculating currencies, sipping at kiosks.

'Did you see George?' she asked.

They were sitting under the bridge, on the steps by the river. It was very peaceful there, and Chako felt detached again. At times his inability to feel things, to get involved seemed arid, at other times like this he was almost cool, desireless and afloat – like the black swans on the blue water.

'I stayed with a man called George and his daughter Anna for a day.'

'Anna. Yes, she would be called that. That was his mother's name. How does she look?'

'A little like you,' Chako said sadly.

'Strange, she must be as old as I was when I left Puthenkavu.'

'Perhaps.'

Sasha didn't notice Chako's silences. She went on ceaselessly as if she had known him for years. He felt detached from her, thinking of the paper he had to present in the afternoon of the next day.

'I was not young or foolish. I was twenty. I knew the fate that I was choosing for myself. I understood that I would suffer, that I would make my people feel pain, that life would have to begin anew and fragmentally. But still, whatever the guilt, this is my life, and I am what I am, and the years have gone by too fast for me to regret. What use would it be anyway, for I cannot go back, or amend things, but must remain where I am.'

He said nothing, remembering a child who wished her mother was dead to avoid understanding an absence without reason.

'We came to Luzern after Azor and I left Bombay. Things were so uncomfortable in India – our two orthodoxies combated us at every turn. So he came to the College of Magic here. It was fun, those early days. After George's rubber fields and the tedium of the rain, and the minuteness of his accounts, I liked it here. Azor was helping to breed unicorns – it failed of course, the goats and the ponies wouldn't get together. Rather awful I suppose if looked at from a Puthenkavu perspective. What do they say about me in the village?'

Chako said nothing. They were looking in at the antique shops which she was thoroughly familiar with. The glass windows were clear and they could see the old beautiful gleaming wood. She knew, without entering, the prices of each artefact, and the period and place from where they had come. They walked down the narrow cobbled lanes, with their seventeenth-century facades and their modern interiors, white lace hanging at the windows, delicate oil lamps at polished desks. It was a world she was completely at home in.

'We've been out for two hours now. Isn't Azor concerned where you are and who you're with?' he asked, looking at that unperturbed, vaguely avaricious face.

'He's never been possessive. He knows infidelity is painful – I don't think either of us could suffer again. Why didn't you marry?'

'I was too busy with one thing or another. Work, I suppose. And then my mother. She's the opposite of you.'

Sasha laughed.

'I could not have married, really. She's so obsessive about me. I get away for a while by planning trips somewhere or the other. She wouldn't tolerate another woman in my life. I think I knew it would be cruelty to marry, the violence between women is painful to bear.'

'George's mother was like that. He should have remained loyal like you. But then there was property to be inherited. When he saw Anna . . . Anna? . . . he said, "An expense." That's all he saw when he first held her. And then Azor came, and he looked at me, and no one had wanted me before. I made coffee for him one day when no one was at home. That's how it began. It's all so long ago. And now George must be forty-eight. Strange, but there it is.'

She pushed her fingers through the short smooth hair. She was extremely, poignantly beautiful, but somehow centreless. He had never met anyone like her, and he felt emptied too – unable to mourn for a lost child in mismatched clothes.

'Would you like to come with us to Rigi? We go by cable car.'

'No,' he said, remembering Anna.

the journey of dispossession

It was raining hard when we reached the church. The reedmats were stained and the women had feet grimed by river sand. It was centuries ago that Puthenkavu had been a coastal village. Now only the sand was there to prove it. It was almost thirty miles inland but when the storms came one was at once reminded of the sea. It was dark inside the church. A lamp fluttered in the centre. I could hardly see the priest in his black robes, but his face, translucent and pale, was uplifted. The golden paten and chalice were in his hands. We were late.

It was true that I had not eaten enough that day. But more than that it was the memory of my brother's wife that disturbed me. She was younger than I, and yet because my brother was older, I had to treat her with deference. Then yesterday my glance had held her and she quickly moved away. Her name was Sarah and Mother alone called her Saramma. My brother did not call her anything. I doubted if he loved her. They say that for many years he had asked Father's permission to marry another girl – beautiful in her way, she had gold earrings that reached her shoulders and a saffron linen cloth over her head.

Her eyes were always rimmed with that black ash girls use, and yes, she was beautiful. They were a rich family for her father was an owner of rubber plantations – there was no getting over the fact that they were Hindus. So it was Sarah who was brought into our house, paying her way really because she came with a large dowry. I think she accepted that Thomas didn't love her, but she was dutiful enough, and Mother became attached to her in a way we all found surprising. Mother, fat, and so ugly, but with the most loving hands, worn and somehow always dirt creased. It was as if she spent her breathing moments tilling in the yard, growing something or another. Sarah was different. I loved her from the moment that I saw her standing in this very church waiting for my brother to marry her.

Last night I went into my brother's room. Sarah was sleeping curled like a small beautiful hooded snake, her hair still coiled at the top of her head. My brother was sprawled on his back on a mat on the other side. I stood over her and after a while she woke, saw me and started. I held her wrists and tried to take her with me, but she would not come. We never spoke.

In the morning she served Father, Thomas and myself our breakfast. Then we all went to church together, except Mother who was planting yams in the back garden. She said she could hear everything from the church very clearly, and would accompany us next week.

In the church as we stood, I looked at Sarah. Her head was bowed and I could see from her face that she was thinking about last night. Thomas stood behind, and Father next to me. The storm blew outside and the chanting of the priest became louder as the wind crashed the wood-green windows. No one moved to shut them. Then Sarah fainted.

Thomas, Father and I did not move. How could we go over to the women's aisle? The priest read from the Evangelion as if he had seen nothing. My father's brother's wife went and picked her up and then with a circle of women around her, I saw them take Sarah out. Our house is next to the church.

When the service was over, Chako of Kadapuram came and stood with us. Thomas had showed no sign of wanting to rush home. Father was doing the parish accounts. It was not my duty to say anything, so I stood with Thomas waiting for him to say something.

'What was it with Sarah?' Chako asked my brother.

'Didn't eat probably,' my brother replied, spitting out his betel leaf juice in a neat noiseless squirt that hit the hibiscus accurately.

'Nothing else?'

'Why don't you ask my mother?'

'Yes, I'll tell Mariamma to do that. Are you coming to the rally tomorrow?'

'Yes, I'll be there.'

'Markose, when are you getting married?' he said looking at me suspiciously.

'When Father says.'

'Well. I'll talk to him. You're growing a beard – that's a bad sign for a young man.'

'I'm in no hurry.'

'No, no ... there is a time for everything under the sun.'

He looked as if he were about to quote a long passage from the Bible, so Thomas quickly asked him to come to our house for coffee. Chakosaar, we well knew, always had coffee with the parish priest, a sign of his status in the village, and the conversation was terminated.

When we sat down for lunch Sarah was not there. 'Saramma is asleep. She's not well,' my mother said as she poured hot fish curry on our rice.

'What is wrong?' my father asked, licking rice off his knuckles.

'A child, I think.'

'Well, the priest will come. Fainting during the Eucharist is not a good thing.'

'It was not during the sacrifice, it was during the Evangelion,' I said.

'Whatever it was, it was a bad sign.'

We continued our meal silently. In the afternoon Father went to see the priest, Thomas went to see his friends at Pathanam, and mother lay down near Sarah. They never saw me as I lay on the other side of the wall on an old mat.

'What is the matter?'

'Thomas doesn't care for me. He still meets that girl.'

'How do you know?'

'From the way he looks at me.'

'When the child comes you will forget all this.'

'I want to go to my mother's house!'

'We'll send you in the seventh month.'

'When are you getting Markose married?'

'I have found a girl for him but she is still young. Why do you cry, Sarah? Having a child is a good thing. You must eat more from now on. No need to help me from tomorrow. Rest now.'

She got up with many groans and then I saw her heading toward the outhouse, where she kept the goats. Her fat body rolled from one side to another. After I saw her busy in her evening chores, I went over to where Sarah was lying.

SARAH:

I saw him standing over me again. His eyes were almost yellow like some forest lion. They burnt me. All night I could not sleep, remembering how he had come to me in the night. Again he will hold my wrist. Again he will raise me. I cannot fight. Thomas loves Shanthamma. And now I carry his child – born of darkness and indifference. Here in this dark room as the seed grows and grows this man will take me. Am I to say nothing?

'What do you want?'

'You.'

'I'll tell Amma.'

'Why don't you tell Thomas.'

'So you heard –'

'One doesn't need to hear to know. Come away with me. We will begin somewhere together. I have loved you from the moment that I saw you. Come with me, Sarah. We will leave this house today if you wish.'

'And the child?'

'It will be like mine.'

'It is not yours.'

'We will have others together.'

'You will hate me later. What will you do if you leave here? You are still a student. This house is yours, I know Achayen will leave it to you. If you leave, Thomas will inherit it.'

'Is Thomas to get everything without even caring for them?'

'Sometimes I wonder why he married me when he cannot even remember my name.'

'Father wanted your money.'

'Well he can have it. Once Amma dies, I shall leave.'

'Can you love me? I won't ask for anything.'

'Love and not ask for anything?'

'Yes.'

'Thomas asks for nothing and I am cursed. Don't talk of love to me. You don't even understand what it means.'

'I crave for you. Thomas doesn't need you.'

'When the child is born he will love me.'

'You are speaking like Amma. Don't you have a mind of your own?'

'My body and my soul are my own. If you touch me once more I'll tell Amma.'

'Amma won't believe you.'

'That is also true. Amma thinks her sons are saints. Get out now. She is coming and it will break her heart if she hears.'

'I will come again.'

I felt deep hatred for all of them. Even for Amma who

loved me like a daughter. I dreamed of running away, of going to some city where no one knew me, of starting life again. This house so prosperous, so comfortable, was seeped in rot, and I, slowly, was becoming like them. It would only be a matter of time before I became like them – pious, churchgoing, kneeling every day on the mats, tilling the earth, sowing the grain and yet running alongside a deep vein of corruption. Father was always dealing with money, Thomas infatuated with a woman he could not marry because of religion, betraying me, Markose full of desire like an adolescent, his eyes sulphur when he looked at me, and yet, so chaste and brown as he watched the chalice raised in the sanctum. And this child I am to carry who will grow and grow and will shatter me.

'Sarah! Sarah! Wake up! The priest has come to see you.'

'I'm coming.'

She washed her face in the cold water from the well. The sky was still grey, the breeze heavy and cold, the wet leaves glistened clean and jewel-like. A thick brown centipede wandered over her foot and she shook it off impatiently. I was sitting on the washing stone waiting for the bath water to heat. She was so self-absorbed she didn't see me. Her face was swollen and the rubies in her ear glinted in the grey light. She was looking at herself in the well. It must have been miserable for her, first to faint in the church, and then to find herself pregnant by Thomas, and then my accosting her.

'Sarah, you'd better hurry up. The priest is waiting for you.'

'Markose, I can't go now. Tell mother I'm collecting the firewood for the coffee and then I'll be there.'

'He doesn't have all that much time – and it's a Sunday too.'

'Well, you talk to him.'

'Talk to the priest? I have no sin burdening me.'

'And I have?'

'All right, I'll tell mother about the coffee.'

When Sarah came to the hall where the old priest was sitting, she had the composed look that Christian women wear almost like a mask – fortitude, patience, humility, readiness to suffer. There was no love in this combination though, and by the light of evening's first candle her face looked almost hard.

'Father, coffee.'

'Yes, I was waiting for you.'

'I am here.'

'Sit down, child.'

She sat at the edge of the bed, the priest sat on the large armchair. His face was thin and grave, large-eyed, his beard silver in the shadows.

'You are not well, I hear.'

'I am all right now.'

'You fainted while I was reading about Jesus and the Samaritan Woman.'

'It was suddenly hot.'

'Hot, when there is a storm blowing the windows down?'

'I felt hot.'

'You felt ashamed to hear of a woman whom Jesus knew to have five husbands?'

'No, I was ill.'

'You had fever? Women do not normally faint in the church. Eliyamma, did the child have fever?'

'No, father. She is in a different way – carrying we think.'

'Ah, that is good news. A baptism in my church soon. Well, why faint? The mother who had such sudden and glad tidings did not faint.'

'Thomas' child is not Yesu.'

'Saramma!' Amma cried.

'No, that cannot be. But you did not faint because of that. There is some other reason. Tell me. I am like your father. I am your father. I have no wife or she should have spoken to you, speak now.'

Sarah got up and walked away. We heard her go into the inner room and then there was the creak of the old wooden bed, the sound of the small flat wooden blade of a window closing.

The priest got up and closed his Bible.

'Your coffee is untouched,' Mother said.

'It is now cold.'

'I will make some fresh.'

'No. I will go now. Send her to confession.'

'She has changed in some way. Such a loving child. It is true some women do not take childbearing well.'

'You are a good mother to tell. Tell Yakob I came.'

* * *

That night I went to Sarah's room again. She came with me. We went to the river and though it was damp from the rain I took her there. In the morning she was gone from the house. We looked everywhere, even in the river. Her parents came to our house and wept. Mother died soon after, Thomas continued to visit his woman, but of Sarah we heard nothing.

shadows painted over

My brother Isak and I had been friends with Manik the painter. Isak was seventeen, and I was twenty when Manik left for America. I often thought about him for I had watched him at work. He would kneel on the ground, his beedi caught between his front teeth, his hands drawing those clear lines with thin brushes which gave you the structures of dew-drops, leaves, shadows of trees – all these things in their minutest detail. One day he loaned me a piece of music. I played the old worn tape, anonymous, with one side blank – and what came forward was music I'd never heard before unless it was in Erewhon. I should have asked him what it was, but admitting ignorance seemed a crime to me then. The music sent me straight onto the moors, though I had never seen any then, and I could hear the wind, I could see the rushes and smell the wild grasses.

Manik was never impatient with us, though often we disturbed him when he was deep at work. He'd just nod, grip his beedi tighter between his square polished teeth, and wave to us to sit in one of those round basket chairs which was about all the furniture he had. Then we would wait for him to finish, to look up. Sometimes he never would emerge from the canvas, and then we'd go quietly, taking care not to creak or shuffle or slide or talk as we left. He understood silence in the way he understood music and I think he painted both. 'The signs of sound, that's my craft,' he said once.

I'm not sure I heard him correctly. Did he say 'science of sound' or 'signs of sound'? I can't really be sure. Except that I wish I had learnt something from him in those eighteen months that we were friends. Perhaps I had – perhaps I learnt that concentration was a technique, and that hands had a life of their own, and one needed to find a balance between discipline and freedom. I never mastered the lesson though.

Like me, Isak loved Manik but he wasn't frightened of him as I was. He would watch as the structure of leaf or rhythm or stone appeared on canvas, sometimes sitting still for eight or nine hours. Manik painted sitting on his haunches without moving. There was a bond between them and they never needed to speak, explain, apologise, remonstrate. I suppose they shared a love for black ink which was a stronger symbiote than blood or semen.

Then father stopped us from going there. He asked us what we could possibly have in common with a man twenty years older than us? If he saw us going there once more he'd break us.

So we stopped going to Manik's house, and sometimes we saw him in the shops, buying those sparse groceries we associated with him. Chicory coffee and arrowroot biscuits. He would smile at us with affection and some amusement. I wonder if he really noticed that we were not visiting him. I was heartbroken for more than a year after the break but Isak was more resilient. He did what all the other boys his age were doing – taking off to America. He lives there with his wife now.

Manik went to America much before Isak. He said New York was like Paris in the 1880s. I always thought of him as rich and happy, almost sixty now, surely. Then I heard that he had died. I couldn't bear the epitaph of his poverty in rich America either. He lived so frugally in India where asceticism had a value. I mourned for him, because he had always been physically very strong. He reminded me of an antelope. He was always listening – rain, water dropping, shadows falling, leaves drying, stones disintegrating, hearts stopping. He could hear things I never saw. What he seemed to see was things alive in nature, and death would have taken him by surprise.

I was used to pain, and to friends leaving me. I was used to the silence that follows when fellow actors became famous, got married, found other sorts of jobs, had babies, left town, found other loves – all the reasons one loses touch with people. But not too many had died on me. I'd always thought I'd see him again. He had loved America, had a whole set of American works, abstracts: and he would look at them with a strange half leaping desire.

Isak and I would peer over Manik's shoulder, breathing down the electric hair at the back of his Doric neck. He was not innocent – who is at thirty-eight? – but he left us hanging about him as gently and subtly as he would moths or idle grasshoppers.

I went to see Isak some years after I had news of Manik's death.

Isak was pleased to see me. It had been all of seven years since we had last met. He sped me through the main streets of Philadelphia, talking all the while. He always felt frightened downtown. 'Blacks,' he said with a conspiratorial wink, with complete disregard for his own jet-skin. His wife had 'good blood and was fashionable' (my mother's description), and she was perfectly content in suburban America.

'Manik died,' I said, while helping myself to roast potato and broccoli soup. Anna was the great American cook. She opened packets the way my mother peeled onions or scaled fish: utter concentration.

'Died?' my brother said, looking over the desiccated green in his large hollow spoon.

'Manik. Our friend. The artist.'

'He's dead? Yes, of course I remember him. I spent hours with him. Do you remember how you used to look? We must have spent hours at his house. He just let us sit there because it meant something to us. I liked him a lot. Anna, what ice-cream?' He had returned to his present.

'Shall I heat another packet of soup?' Anna asked.

'This broccoli must have been grown when dinosaurs were about,' I said.

'Don't be mean, Susa. Fresh fish smells and meat is so bloody and the chickens probably artificially inseminated.

All America is eating broccoli. The President loves it, why can't you?' Isak was looking warily at me.

'Okay, but while I'm here I'm going to cook for you.'

'Thanks,' my brother said.

'Susa, why don't you get a nose job while you're here?' Anna asked. She was protective over her supermarket choices of granola, baked beans and asparagus.

'What on earth for?' I said placidly, for I am as ugly as she is beautiful.

'Well, your nose is so Roman, darling. I'm sure Isak can afford it. He's just bought me a second car.'

'Anna, I play character roles. I can't afford to look pretty or dumb.'

'How's the theatre doing?' my brother asked.

'Street theatre mainly,' I said, bitter that the grand conflagration between Anna and me had been deflected by my brother who loved us both.

I didn't help them with the washing. I could hear them arguing over which ice-cream to take out. Manik seemed far away, back into our childhood in Delhi. He would have encouraged that. I could almost hear him saying: 'Hey Sioux? What's new?'

snakes and fishes

It was raining. There was a sea of black umbrellas, all open, all moving. Their ribcages gleaming copper in the dusk. Occasionally one could see the river, but it was just a glimpse, through a dark mass of moving people.

What in hell was I doing here? My teeth were cold and clamped together. My clothes were soaked, my bags were heavy and I had no umbrella. Then I felt someone holding my arm. It was Philip. We walked together silently for a while, barefoot on the sand. The people swirled about us. I hadn't seen him for thirty years! And this was a bishop's funeral. Philip had always been in the classroom when I collected my things. We were always the last to leave – I was slow and disorganised, and he in charge of putting things in order. He had a way of looking which was typically his – sharply, steadfastly. It always unnerved me because it implied an objectivity of diagnoses.

'Who was the Bishop to you?' he asked me, the way he always spoke, curtly, suddenly.

'My father's friend. They studied together. And to you?' I answered.

'My mother's brother.'

'That close? I never knew.'

'Come back with us to the house. My mother will want to see you after all these years.'

'I can't. I'm going to Allapuzha. I must see my father today.'

'How old is he now? Seventy?'

'Eighty.'

'He had you when he was thirty-three then. How many children do you have?'

'None,' I said, smiling. 'I never married.'

'What! I always imagined you with a thin bony husband with curly hair and ironed shirts.'

'You thought of me.'

'Often. It's a pity you had no dowry, and then you had ambitions. We would not have lasted together for long.'

'You always were so shameless and cruel.'

Philip let go my arm. His hair was grey in places, and his square jaw was resolute.

'So did you become a doctor?' he asked me. He had remained on his father's land. No degrees.

'Sure.'

'And where did you go?'

'I went to Bombay.'

'Bombay. What's it like?' he asked idly. We had reached the main road. The river glinted behind us – neither blue nor grey nor black – just spangled by the lights of the roadside.

'Busy.'

'Sounds like Europe.'

'Been there?' I started laughing.

'No. Who's got the time? But I watch films.' He rolled

up his starched linen sleeves. His wrists were very thin and the bones were very prominent.

'What about you? Did you marry?' I said as clinically as possible.

'Of course I did. You know I was not destined to study like you. I grew tapioca. Export variety.'

'Tapioca.' I looked at him in horror.

'Why not? Don't you eat tapioca and fish any more?'

'I haven't eaten tapioca or any sort of yam since I left home.'

'Come home then. There's the car – my wife and my children – come and meet them.'

'No, I'll go. I don't want to meet them.'

'Forgotten your Malayalam?'

'What are we speaking in?'

He turned his face away towards the stream of traffic coming our way. The second of the funeral cars stopped, and he got in. He slammed the door shut and looked straight ahead. His wife was very lovely – small, squat, sturdy with a round face and laughing eyes. His daughters were in the back, sprawled across their mother. The funeral was over, they had fallen back into what looked like a general and normal state of contentment and ease. She had bangles from her wrist to her neck. In all probability she never took them off. Tapioca Export Limited. Philip was doing well.

It was not strange really the quick intimacy we had fallen into. I may be protesting too much, but it was not sexual, and it was not because it was Philip. Men always talked to me with an ease – not flirtatious – but a closeness that came from the belief that I, as a physician, understood their bodies, anonymously and immediately. Bare all. I am forty-seven! Not such a great age – halfway through life, since everyone lives to a great age in my family. The longevity was a charm, not a curse. All the men and women in both Father's line and Mother's line had this great gift of a long life. How did they spend it? Reading newspapers and the Bible, looking up for a moment when over-ripe jackfruit dashed to the ground in some nearby field.

I wanted to see my father. He would be waiting for me across that huge expanse of water, waiting for news of his friend, now interred, who had studied with him sixty years ago – Mar Raphael.

I caught the Fast Passenger from the junction. We went hurtling through narrow country roads, falling into potholes and rolling out with amazing ease. My fellow travellers were surprised to see me alone – a woman, at night, in a Fast Passenger! – but I sat comfortably listening to the rain drumming against the tarpaulin curtains. I felt exhausted by my meeting with Philip. No reason, really. I just felt thrown into the vortex of some shamed, half-stated desire. Marriage was a rational business – that he would do well, with the quietness and cunning of old practice: marry good blood, money, acquiescence.

I took out my cigarettes from my squelchy leather handbag. How it had rained! I didn't look about, but I could sense the astonishment about me: 'Cigarettes, no secret!' I knew I ought not to smoke, but then what the hell! My patients, smokers at the end of the line themselves, didn't object either to my rasping bedside tone or the raw odour of tobacco around me. Father would of course. I shuddered, and looked out of the window, twirling up the heavy tarpaulin as best as I could. The rain slanted in. Everything was hazy, but the red-tiled roofs came across in the dim lights washed and clean.

We reached Allapuzha at eight in the evening. The house had been newly painted. The coconut trees had started to flower. The door was shut. I rang the bell, and sat on the mosaic ledge which circled the balcony. The smell of bitter lemons was in the air. The rain had stopped, not even a drizzle. I could hear the dog barking at the back. Was my father already asleep? Oh God. It was difficult waking him up once he'd gone to bed. Then I saw him through the iron grille: he was shuffling to the door, tying his white linen dhoti, his face crushed and wrinkled from sleep and age.

'Is this the time to come home?'

'It's only eight o'clock. The moon hasn't even risen.'

'Exactly . . . Look at it! It's night.'

'Why do you go to sleep so early? Aren't you glad to see me?'

Suddenly he smiled – his teeth were crooked and yellow, but his beautiful brown eyes were alight.

'Come in. I wake up at four, you know, in the morning, and then there's so much to do the whole day. If your mother were alive I wouldn't be so tired. Look, have you eaten? There's some bread and butter. Fresh bread from the bakery. Go wash. And don't give the dog any.'

I put my bags into the cupboard. The teak wood was thick and old, the latch was a solid block which ran across the length of the two doors. I hid my cigarettes behind my books. Father always went through everything I had – a habit of surveillance he'd kept on from my childhood.

There was no point expecting things to be different. Neither he nor I believed that I had been around for more than forty years. In some ways I would always be a child: talented, skilled professionally, but unable to mature. Luckily it was not noticeable enough to matter.

I slept the sleep of the exhausted – dead to the world in the pitch dark room where no moon shadows came. I loved that room. It had been mine since birth. I had opened my eyes to the thick brown ceiling from which hung the brown wicker baskets of lights. Moths hurtled about, with dull satin wings. The darkness always enclosed one, and the fragility of life always appeared in stark contrast to the teak laid room. No more children of our family were to be born in this room. I hadn't married, my brothers and sisters had never been born. I lay there as the clean morning light filtered in, listening to the voices of people who had inhabited this room, lain together in love or enmity, marriages captured in circles of emotion.

I went out to speak to Father. He was raking leaves.

'So. Why have you come home at this time of the year? Want money to set up a practice?'

'No. I thought I'd see you.'

'There's nothing wrong with me. Nothing right either. Tell me, do you really get patients?'

'I'm the best.'

'You always were absent-minded. Are you sure you don't leave things behind in bellies?'

I shifted weight from one foot to another like I did when I was small. Now he would ask me whether I cooked at all. I was longing for coffee and cigarettes. The smell of dry leaves, scented with margosa and mango was terrific.

The sky was clean blue, not a cloud. I thought of Philip. There had been something troubling about the way he fitted back into my life, everything as familiar as well-trod memory. He'd thought of me often and I of him. An absence of thirty years had made no difference. Desire, like an old shoe, fitted snugly, cocooning and familiar. If need was trite, inaccessibility could be a demon. We could not have made a life together – that was clear enough – but that did not stop him from looking at me, or I at him. No guilt either – I wasn't going to moan about the thoughts that crossed my head. They were free to come and go, I barely glanced at anything that distracted me from the central principle of my life – my work.

I made tea slowly – no coffee to be found. Mother drank coffee, and Father drank tea. My back hurt, my head was heavy. I felt slowed down and sad. Then I remembered one morning, decades ago. It was inextricably tied in with my avoidance of Philip, of being seventeen, of fear, cowardice, the sheer hopelessness that life filled me with even then. Nothing to hold on to, nothing to believe in, everyone a stranger. Things hadn't really changed, I was older now, that's all.

All the rooms in Father's house were kept empty except three. He believed in frugality. That February, Mother had been away at Maramon, where our Church holds a prayer meeting on the river bank. It was early summer. I had come back from Medical College – everything looked green. Father had kept the water tanks at the back always filled. He would leave the hose-pipe on all night, and the fish would swim about in happy shoals. During the day, the sun would evaporate almost one-third of the water.

They were catfish. Have you ever seen them? They have shiny backs, rheumy and smooth, which shine in the sun. They have long whiskers, cat's whiskers. We don't eat these fish. Maybe they're all right to eat if one was desperately hungry – that is, poor – but usually we don't. I'd seen them once hurtling along in a fast-flowing clear temple stream somewhere in Kashmir, rolled along by a current, with no control of their life. They were fed by pilgrims, and I remember touching them through the cold crystal of that fervent water.

These catfish which Father bred were different. They were fat and placid, and loved the sun. The water was always shadowed and green, mossy, and from nowhere at all large snails had attached themselves to the sides of the tank. Were there water-lilies? I don't recall. The sun would run into the water through the leaf-green guava trees and the fat bodies of the fish would display themselves. Suddenly there would be schools of them. When had they spawned? I was always curious about how these fish actually spent their days. They hoped for food, and ripples of excitement would pattern the water whenever I arrived. I would put my feet into the water as I sat on the topmost step, and immediately my feet would be nibbled by perennially hungry fish.

One day, as I sat immersed up to my knees in the moulting water, I saw the snake. I leaped up and ran in, shivering. I looked through the slats of the bedroom windows. It was looking back at me. It was only a water-snake.

'Father!' I began to scream. 'A snake. A snake.'

Father came rushing out with a bamboo pole. 'Where?' he cried, his frail body trembling.

'There.' I pointed to the snake looking out from the water. Its eyes were black.

'Oh,' said Father. 'It's only a water-snake.'

'Please chase it away.'

'I said, it's only a water-snake.'

'I know it's only a water-snake, but I'm scared.'

Father was bored, angry. I thought he was going to repeat 'It's only a water-snake' but he stopped himself and said, 'It will eat a couple of fish and go away.' He was anxious to get back to planting a quinine bush someone had gifted him.

'Call Pappu Pillai,' I said, adamant.

'What on earth for? Say his name and it costs me twenty rupees. Why should I call him? I don't have any work for him.'

'Please call him. Please chase away the snake. I'm frightened. This snake will call his mate. They'll have children. They'll come into our house. They'll hang from the rafters. Please call Pappu Pillai.' Tears were running down my face. In those days I could cry at will.

'All right,' said Father, looking at me in disgust. He yelled over the wall for Pappu Pillai who was washing down my uncle's cowshed.

Pappu Pillai sauntered in. He was around seventy, with a face out of a colonial gazetteer on *Castes and Tribes of Travancore*. He constantly smoked a beedi, and didn't seem to notice, as we all did, that he was dying of cancer.

'What is it? What do you want?'

'There's a snake in the water tank.'

'So?'

'We want you to chase it away,' I said.

'It'll go by itself.'

'Please, Pappu Pillai. I'll ask Father to give you twenty-five rupees to get rid of the snake.' I looked for Father: he had disappeared.

'Twenty-five rupees to kill a snake. Even if you gave me a thousand, ten thousand, I wouldn't kill a snake.'

'Don't kill it. Just send it away.'

'Stone it? I couldn't stone it. Catch it, I can't. Bind it, trap it . . . no, I can't.'

'Please, Pappu Pillai, do something. Adichu Viddu. Beat it away.' I was desperate.

'All right I will. Ayrichu Viddam. I'll let it loose,' he said slowly.

'What? What will you do?'

'You'll see.' He spat some bloody phlegm, dusted tobacco powder off his hands. Then he went to the wall, where the stopper of the tank was ensconced and pulled it hard.

I happened in a moment. The water spilled out, swilled out. The fish all flew out in the current through the hole, rather like those hapless catfish, representative of souls in the clear streams of that Northern mountain temple. They died in the sun. There were *thousands* of them. I couldn't bear to see their death agony, but I could not look away either. Their murky moss-coated black backs began to shine luminescently as they died. Thousands of eyes begged me for life as they fought in the grass, singly and collectively for a bubble of water.

'I'll collect my money later,' said Pappu Pillai, as he went back to my uncle's house.

Father said nothing to me, as he came and stood beside

me, watching the thousand glittering bodies turning in the sun like wind-blown mica. The snake was still in the tank, slithering out to the centre, where small patches of water remained on the rough cement surface.

'Jesus said, "Be wise as serpents and innocent as doves."'

'I'm sorry.'

'Don't you know that Pappu Pillai will never harm a snake?'

My uncle came across. He looked at the still, brown serpent in the empty tank.

'So is he dead or not?' he asked me.

'No,' I said.

'I'll do it.'

My father went back to the front garden. Uncle broke a stout stick from the guava tree and killed the snake, as neutrally as if he were hitting a coconut on a rock.

'Dangerous things, snakes, even water-snakes. Just fear can kill,' he said and threw its mangled body near an ancient mildewed wall, covering it with earth.

Pappu Pillai never spoke to me the whole summer. After a month I saw a peepal tree growing where Uncle had buried the snake. It was coincidence, an airborne seed, but Pappu Pillai felt that I could be forgiven. As for the fish, they merged with the rich loam earth.

fire drill

Sainsbury's, the English store had just opened – Belfast was becoming cosmopolitan. People took taxis from all over town to glut on strange salads, chocolates and cheese. Europe had opened its borders: one could spend a day in Milan, a fortnight in Scotland, ten days in Portugal, almost at no cost. Belfast was going to become a culture centre. In the post office one could only get one kind of stamp – the young Queen's sculpted head, forever twenty-five, forever beautiful. Sometimes in the street, a copper coin with a harp and 'Eire' written on it would gleam, but it was only for a moment – trapped in the rain, polished by sun and tarmac till it shone with rainbow colours.

There were flower sellers in every corner, and balloons floating in clusters, and the dim grey of northern skies. In the dark downpour, people smiled at each other and a hundred different fragrances mingled with cigarette smoke blue in the dusk.

At the University of Belfast, the turrets and spires rose to another sky, blue unclouded, time stopped still. The community kept protest alive by teaching political theory and keeping records of the Troubles. I was a student of Gemmology, but I specialised in the violin in the Department of Ethnomusicology set up by the famous John Blacking. His presence was electric – though he had been dead now for seven years.

I was playing a difficult raga the day there was a fire drill. The alarm went off – pure pain – that clanging, screaming, yowling, hooting, electric gong of a bell – that screamed down into every neuron. Doors banged and people ran. I didn't want to leave. I was halfway through riyaz and it was suddenly pelting outside – blue skies transformed by showers – the fire was warm in me, that curling, winding flame that arises when one's playing. Barefoot, I picked up my things. I ran out into the street. It was freezing outside, the rain had turned to ice, and my violin was without its case. I ran in again, but the burly fire officer pulled me out saying, 'No personal possessions please.'

'My passport,' I yelled, lying. He let me go. And then all the doors sealed behind me. I couldn't get out.

Luckily, Adrian Cavanagh was late too – he was carrying his monograph on the Evolution of Seaweed, and we managed to get out, this time with my shoes on and the violin in its black leather case. We got stared at by everybody, but Cavanagh, his red scarf trailing in the breeze, just bared his teeth in that distancing scholarly smile he had. The Head of Ethnomusicology pretended he'd never seen me in his life and took a head count. Who was missing? No one was. I was the only one without socks and I was freezing.

'Sumana,' he suddenly said, 'I'd like to speak to you.'

I could see trouble. The burly security officer was grinning and I felt like a schoolboy reading comics in the games period, hauled over the coals for not doing gymnastics in the rain.

The Head of Department had green eyes exactly like his wife, and they both drove off every evening together in a car that matched their eyes. Inviolate, beautiful and bad-tempered. Sometimes I saw them quarrelling companionably at the crossroads, both of them staring each other out, and sending off sparks at anyone who dared to intrude into the privacy of their love in the hurtling traffic.

Of course I was jealous. I wanted love like that in my life. Sometimes I wished the violin had never found me. It fitted against my body like a man, its smooth mahogany had a fragrance, again masculine, permeated by the intense moisture of some craftsman's fingers; it exuded pine scents every time I rubbed it down and the horse hair was taut against my fingers. When I played, fire uncurled in my belly and lust and wisdom swirled in my blood like Eve's serpent.

We climbed up the red-carpeted stairs in total silence – three floors up to his room bare as a monastic's, with books lining the shelves six feet high. He was a big, beautiful man, with the famous Irish lilt in his voice, and a way that was so charming I immediately wanted to be in some vaulted church with sharp-edged coloured glass fitted together to strain the light. Scholastics God that he was, he solved problems by signing his name large at the bottom of franked paper, and thud the seal went below. Energy and compassion mixed together with sudden gales of laughter.

I shut the door carefully behind me. One never got invited to the sanctum unless there was a crisis. I tried not to look happy, but was distraught enough to drop the books on his table without going anywhere near there.

'What in hell do you mean sauntering downstairs ten minutes after everyone else is out? When that alarm goes you leave everything, you don't get into the lift, you don't stop to pick up your lipstick or your tights (he said this in the clearly misogynist style of men who had had feminist mothers in the 1940s). 'You land downstairs in thirty seconds flat, is that understood?'

'Yes!' I said, totally numb. And then I was dismissed. Patriarchy was alive and well, we all submitted to his gentleness if we were good, and his hauteur and bad temper if we had offended him.

One day I went up to his flat uninvited. It was cluttered with papers and books – strewn all over the floor like confetti. He was pleased to see me and took off my silk coat and settled me on a sprawling sofa. Then he went into the kitchen to make coffee, cursing inwardly because I had disturbed his writing. When he appeared with two fragrant cups, he had completely recovered from the interruption and immediately began to ask me if I was comfortable in Belfast, and whether the money was adequate. Officialese hung between us like a heavy cloak, like a chaperone. I was desperately in love with him and perhaps it shadowed my eyes, palimpsest of many other loves, because I had never been able to distinguish between lust and love. My body had its needs and I responded to anyone who could quieten it. Sometimes I would walk miles in the night longing for the moon and then it would

rain and I would limp home, grateful for the warmth of
blankets.

Simon immediately began talking about his wife and
his children who were in their house in the country. His
love was so gentle, so delicately balanced between the
hundred books strewn about and his family that I did not
dare disturb that careful equilibrium, and having finished
my coffee I went out into the dusk.

Yellow bushes, like sunshine, gleamed in the foggy dull
streets. A bird called, the light was almost gone. Suddenly
I saw the thin moon and knew that it had been there for
millions of years. I liked it here, I felt free and cold and
dizzy. My body was constrained by coats and jackets, but
my head was swimming all the time like an early sea with
its first plankton.

The man in the bank wrote out all my cheques for me,
spelt my name correctly, gave me his thin elegant silver
pen to sign with. Then he asked me to go out with him.
He had a face like paper frozen in ice, and eyes blue like
still lakes and everything about him was like the winter.
His thin frame once exposed would show up like the
branches of trees. We walked for a long while near the
river with its water birds, brown and speckled and unafraid
of the icy water. He held my hand, complete strangers
that we were as we stepped on the flat white stones.

'You have arranged marriages in India even now?'
'Yes.'
'Women like you go to bed with a complete stranger?'
He'd understood the excitement of the arranged

marriage. It was just that, surely, that made husband and wife lovers of such stability? The dangers were there too of course, and who did not know of those? But what made it work was the cheerful way in which partners were chosen by father, mother, grandfathers, grandmothers, uncles, aunts and cousins to the seventh degree. Everyone sitting over teacups wondering whether they should write to 'Engineer recently returned from States, own business, own house, own car, looks for fair, convent-educated bride with homely habits.'

'We have those too, but we put them in ourselves. Tall man with brown hair and blue eyes, WLTM short, thin girl with GSOH.'

'What's that?'

'Good social outgoing habits.'

'I hate going out. I hate meeting people.'

'But you're here with me now,' he said smiling.

'Yes.'

He took out his cigarettes, which he rolled himself. The army trucks rolled along – fine thin young faces vulnerable as newly-hatched chicks looked out from the cages of machine guns. They should have been playing the violin in neat bedrooms with new satin sheets and velvet curtains. Instead death spilled their guts, or they spilt someone else's in the dark streets of the slums. The hatred was slow and still, and sometimes deep and flowing, but nothing was spoken. In the lovely neighbourhoods of South Belfast, nobody cared a damn. Cherry trees blossomed, schools of runners ran past in shoes that cost two hundred pounds and saved their knees from jerks and shocks, the fragrance of hot bread and Brazilian coffee followed one about, terriers and pugs chased early bees, and the spice-fragrant red lilies uncurled in glasshouses.

He lived in a house from whose window one could see the lights of the hill. He rang the bell and his father opened the door, thin like his son, with the northern cold in his frame, a cold which was passed down generation to generation by the trouble it took to stay that way. We are like that too with the turbulence of our rivers which hurtle and our sun which burns, stamping us in everything that we do.

'Violinist from India,' Alan said.

'Welcome to Belfast,' the old man said, shaking my hand in the way old people do, cold firm hands, briefly held and then detached. How intimate to shake hands. We never do, back home! Sometimes in the halls where I play people hold my hand longer than necessary and I feel like I am trapped in a mesh.

'How long are you here for?'

'A week. I'm planning to go to the Giant's Causeway tomorrow.'

'With my son?'

'Oh no! We just met.'

'My father was born in India, you know. He used to tell us about it. Shimla of course, and the church at Kashmiri Gate. Is it close to Kashmir? I'm so sorry you're having such troubles.'

'The Troubles. That's our story,' Alan said, taking his father by his arm and gently steering him toward the living room. He settled the old man in, filled his pipe. I sat across him with the daffodils striking my eyes in the long twilight. They were in a dark purple crystal vase.

'Your wife?' I asked.

'She died many years ago. I brought Alan up myself – did a pretty good job too. I had no desire to marry again. She was very small and Alan was big like I am. I think it was difficult for her – the weight – I don't know. We never met during labour. I believe they allow husbands in nowadays? To hold the wife's hand?'

'I don't know.'

'Don't want marriage and children?'

'I'm a traveller, a musician. I can't stay.'

'I'm so old now. Eighty-six this year. So whatever I say to you, it is innocent. Have you a caste?'

'No. My grandfather says we became Christians when St Thomas the Apostle of Jesus came to India.'

'Oh, like our St Patrick. Do you know we have no snakes because he chased them away?'

'We have loads of snakes. People even wear them around their neck.'

'Nothing wrong with snakes. They have every right to be around. You're really pretty. Don't give yourself to Alan. He'll make you passive, bear children, stop wandering the world . . .'

'Nothing wrong with that, is there?'

'Surely not if you life it, want it. He'll want hot meals, sex every day, twice on Sundays, scrub his bath after him and clean shirts out every day.'

'Stop it,' I screamed, getting fed up of the old man.

He retired behind his newspaper, laughing.

Alan came in with tea that smelt of bitter things. I wanted to give him some of the clear brown liquid we drank in India. They screwed it up here with their twists of lime and thyme. Every time I drank tea I got mad; it did more for me than the Guinness, because this tea was adulterated with flowers and juices of strange kernels, they could put anything in tea, even resin of pine.

'Would you like to see my room?'

'Yes.'

He looked at my throat with the thick silver chains crafted by some tribal metalsmith for the woman he loved. It had a pattern of leaves, each one different from the other, and a primeval forest recorded itself in the imprint of silver and fire. A sudden crashing anger hit his eyes. I understood then what his father meant. If I were ever to accept this man I would be enslaved forever, he would own me, define every moment of my day. But I still wanted him.

When we stopped making love the sky outside was blue, early morning clear and inky. He took me home. I loved his intensity, his coldness, his passion. I knew I'd never meet another man like him again.

'When do you leave for India?'

'Next week, this time.'

'Do you want to do this again?'

'No.'

'Why not?'

'Because I think I love you.'

'That's just the reason I asked you.'

'I said I don't want to. I hate pain. I hate leaving you.'

'You don't have to, you know. You could live with me.'

'We don't even know each other.'

'Make me some coffee. I want to talk to you.'

I opened the door. The cats were about, they had upset

everything – ripped newspaper, clawed down a curtain, turned over a vase. The water dripped down from the side table onto the red carpet with black tulips.

'I'll help you clean up. Get me a mop.' He bent down, crumpling newspaper. He had white hands, beautiful fingers. He hadn't been used to counting money because he'd counted my seven hundred pounds three times at the bank before he'd got it right. He was more used to farmers asking for large loans, which he cleared depending on their assets. And then I had been sent to him because my cheques needed his attention. I wasn't going to suffer. This man needed a wife who wore tailored suits, gold earrings, a perfume called Opium, whom he could take out to stockbrokers' dinners.

I watched helplessly as he put the room to order. His father had said Alan will pulverise you, domesticate you – but no, he didn't, he cleared up after me.

'Are you always so helpless?' he asked abruptly.

'No, at home I'm not. I cook, I clean, I do everything on my own.'

'Get the coffee then.'

I went into the kitchen. I looked all over. I found the beans and ground them, and set the filter going. I watched the sky with its streaks of white. My neighbour's sons, Indian like me, were polishing their silver-grey car. Sometimes the older boy looked straight across at me and there was an intensity, an anguish, a burning that frightened me. He missed India: he knew I was going back, he knew I was going home, he devoured me. He had been born here, and was now more Irish than Indian – but there was enough of language, colour and religion in him that

caused that craving, .
looked at me.

a boy's love, with which he

It was half an hour befor.

'That took a long time. Wha, ght the coffee out.
'I was looking at the sky.' you doing?'
'Listen, I have to leave for work no.

n late. I'll pick
you up at five-thirty.'

'It won't work. We run on different speeu.

'I'm not some clock. I want you, didn't you u, erstand
that? I would not have taken you to meet Father if it were
not so. I would have taken you to a hotel, slept with you
on an alien bed.'

'We only met yesterday. I don't want bondage. I don't
want to marry. I need to be moving. I can't stay in your
beautiful house with the ivory lace curtains your mother
chose.'

'Don't talk about my mother to me. I want you to be
waiting for me at five-thirty.'

He drove off so fast that I could smell the rubber smoking on the tar.

Of course I wasn't there at five-thirty. I caught a bus
out further north, to the Giant's Causeway – several buses
actually, in the cold fog and drizzle. I loved it – my face
froze, and my hair frizzled with the damp. I travelled with
six Spanish women. They took me in, with all the warmth
and chatter of twenty-year-olds. We travelled for miles with
the steel-grey of water, the bare spines of trees, the damp
green of the valleys.

The Causeway was an ancient throne – the water
splashed on it, and its six-shaped stones, cylindrical, like
an organ, grew outwards into the sombre sky.

something barely remembere

the sea, and suddenly for

I stood there lookin... lling my Spanish friends of
no reason at all I st... ps, and a Spanish armada. They
golden rings and co... sea was still, and yet emanating out
nodded in silenc... till and quiet love of bones that had
towards us was... ells. I was telling them of what I had seen
turned into s... useum, of the sadness I had felt at seeing
at the Ulste... those bea... ful golden things – but suddenly the sea spoke
to us ar... told us more. Later a guide told us that it was right
here that the Spanish ship had crashed, mistaking the
Causeway for a lighthouse, for a port – who knows what?

It was a relief to go back to Belfast with its low hills and
its cherry trees, and all those silent locked churches with
stained glass opaque to the outside. The sun was shining
and the pistachio-coloured domes of the Town Hall were
as blatant as ever. Old people fed the pigeons, and the
children were everywhere buying balloons and eating out
of glinting plastic bags. The pubs were open, and black
thick Guinness was foaming out of crystal mugs.

I went to the bank to close my account. Alan looked
through me and drank his coffee and smoked his cigarettes and played with his computer. A woman with gleaming red lips handled my papers and said she hoped I
would return to Belfast. I said, 'Yes. I'm interested in Celtic
jewellery.' Alan looked up and for a moment I thought
he would speak to me but then he squinted his eyes as
the smoke curled up and ripped up papers ferociously.
Then he got up and disappeared into his streamlined
executive's office and I flew the next day.

*   *   *

I needed to recover from my feelings for Alan which engulfed everything so instead of continuing violin performances in New Delhi, I went on to Allapuzha, in Kerala.

Mother lived in a grand house. Not her own, nor my father's. It was a legacy from my grandfather, who had been an iron merchant. I was fond of the house. It gave me a sense of impending doom – I always felt, lying under its eaves, that some day surely I must die. I was assured of my mortality which, given my state of mind, seemed a welcome idea.

That summer it did not rain. I waited for the soft hush, the patter, the drumming of rain – but nothing happened. A tremendous rage started to rise within me – I felt that I had nowhere to go, trapped by sunlight. The heavy iron-grilled windows stared back at me. I had never noticed them before. The sun blazed and dried things copper. Everything seemed to burn down into a flame-coloured death. My mother went about as usual – calm, reticent, afraid to speak to me for she could see molten eyes like my father's staring out of my head. As a child I had been attached to her because she protected me from his rages. Now, without him, we both had solidly different identities. She spent her day ensuring that I did not work – a forced imposition of leisure made sure that I had no place but to lie staring out at an unreal blue sky. This was what she called 'your holiday'.

I went to the beach often – a wild and surly sea. It was black and the sand was white. Shells glimmered here and there. The clouds were strange shapes, offering themselves to Rorschachian interpretations. I felt the sense of being useless drain away. I could look at the sea for hours, the water piling up and breaking free to hit the white sand. Its blackness against the dark blue and orange sky was more than I could bear. I longed to disappear within it.

When I returned home, wet and sandy, my mother never asked what I'd been about. Walls of silence separated us – she was immersed in her 'duties' as she called the selfless devotion she had shown my father in the worst of years. There was a gentleness about her, a failure so penetrating in its silence that I felt embarrassed. In her house, alone and independent and utterly self-sufficient, she had in my presence turned herself into a caretaker, a soulless menial quality which made me dread her. I knew that when I was away, she would recover her own sense of being, and I counted the days to my return to the city – my spinning, scintillating life which had so enervated me that I could no longer feel.

'What will you eat for dinner?'

'Omelette.'

'But I've cooked rice and fish and cabbage.'

'Then why ask me?'

All our conversations ended at dead-ends. We slid into a silence which held no meaning whatsoever. When she thought herself unobserved her face glowed, as if she were alone peacefully again, in a silvery old age.

At the beach the next day, it began to rain. The sea was blacker than ever, more beautiful than I had ever seen it, and incredibly the sky darkened to reflect the sea. It was only four o'clock. I got soaked. I returned home and sat on the balcony, steaming in the sudden hot fluorescent light of a tropical afternoon.

The bell rang – it was a harsh vibratory sound and I sprang up and went to the gate. For a moment I thought it was my father, but of course it was not. It was a beggar, slight and dishevelled with large strange bloodshot eyes which shone with some unidentified passion.

'Where's your mother?' he asked in a strangely familiar tone.

'Sleeping. What do you want?'

'I used to live here. I'm not an ordinary beggar.'

'What?' I said, sleepy with the afternoon's warm soaking in sea and rain and sweat.

'I am not an ordinary beggar,' he repeated.

There was a strange odour of fresh medicines and oils about him, also a decaying, a dreadful passion to live.

'Go away. We've given enough to beggars today.'

'You've never given me anything. Where's your mother?'

My mother came out and started screaming. 'Go away. I hate you. I can't stand the sight of you. Why do you keep disturbing me? Who said you could keep coming here? You came last month too.'

The man became instantly alert. He had met her before, evidently, had tormented her and was instantly awake to the possibility of endless torment ahead.

'I've never been here before,' he said in a smooth pleasant way.

'You came last month, and the month before that. You keep telling me that you're sick . . .'

The man had got as far as the balcony, while we were arguing. He sat down on the red stone seat, crossed his legs, straightened his back and stared back at us with those demonic glittering golden brown eyes.

'I'm not going,' he said very quietly.

My mother went back into the house, suddenly old and defeated, frightened of the beggar whose obduracy was only a type, but represented decades of a specific domestic order. The beggar and I stared at each other. Affection began to shine in his eyes as he listened to me, a shining pride, as if I was his daughter who lectured well to august audiences. I wasn't saying anything very sensible.

'You shouldn't beg! Everyday we give money to all kinds of people – without legs, arms, headless lepers, even failed Marxists who want heart transplants. It's very difficult. Why don't you go and get a job. Just go. I'm sure by evening you'll have a job!'

'Who'll give me a job? What job?' The sneer, the smile, the contempt, the fanatical eyes – all so dreadfully familiar, except that my father had always owned thirty shirts at a time, including a lavender one with a white collar and gleaming mother-of-pearl buttons. I understood my mother's panic.

I gave him a rupee. He got up with amazing agility to take it from me, but when he saw it was a single coin, he sat back again as if he was shocked, ravaged by my lack of charity.

'Where's your mother?' He wiped his eyes with the end of his ragged linen sarong. 'She gives money to all sorts of useless fellows – perfectly healthy – who come to the door. But me, she won't even look at me.' He whipped

himself into an all too familiar frenzy, gloating, vit-
uperative.

'How your mother hates me. Didn't you hear her?
Didn't you hear what she said? She would love to cut my
fingers' (he began to saw his right fingers with his left
wildly) 'and rub salt into them. Where is she?'

I gave him two rupees more. He stopped to put them in
a fold of loincloth. My mother appeared with five rupees.

'Give it to him,' she said tiredly.

'You give it to him.'

When Mother gave the money, the man suddenly
relaxed all his muscles, an almost comic lassitude marked
his face and he went away – he was no ghost, he was just
an irrational memory trace.

I played the violin again that day. And Mother listened
and held me close when I had finished. Suddenly I felt
she was no longer embarrassed by my unorthodox life,
my wild uncircumscribed existence. Then she said, 'We'll
go to the church tomorrow and you can meet everyone.'

'No thanks,' I said, feeling salt in the inner hollow of
the case, fingers numb with the hours. All our different
kinds of devotion make up existence and bell tones are
distinct for each one of us.

kidnapped in Casablanca

We had made love as silently as cats in the large room with glass windows. The low hills outside were grey blue in the morning light and we could hear the squirrels on the roof.

'Who's going to make toast?' he asked.

'You,' I said, looking for my slippers under the bed, 'I'm off for a walk.'

I felt the wind against my body – a cold dry wind which fused with the moist sea air curiously. I could smell the fruit – the olives, the oranges, the green almonds. Somewhere close by was the desert, but closer still was the blue Atlantic.

'Where is the sea?' I asked all the children I met, for Paulo had said, 'Don't talk to strangers.'

They laughed and shook their heads, speaking back to me in Arabic or French. I walked through the main part of town, listening to the mystical Andalusian chants, watching out for the strangers my husband had warned me about. I was the stranger, not they. Why was he always so afraid for me?

I had met him less than a year ago at a friend's house.

He was so gentle; we were married in no time at all. His shoes were always polished, his hair never wind-ruffled and his shirts were deep jewel colours. He treated the rich who lived on health foods, sprouts grown on shining metallic paper and lime-curdled freaky cheeses. I was never excited when I was with him, his aura of calm always lent itself to me. I enjoyed that more than anything.

I didn't find the sea. I came back to our rooms to find the table laid – yes, with check cloth and napkins, thick Casablanca orange juice and bitter coffee and bread and butter. Paulo was good at these things. He'd eaten already and there was not a crumb on the table.

'I'm off. And don't talk to strangers if you go out again.'

'Your conservatism is so dull. Am I supposed to find a lover? Be kidnapped?'

'With you one never knows,' he said smiling. He walked out shutting the door so softly that I yelled 'goodbye' to break the silence. Somewhere inside me I knew we needed each other and we would stay together till our separate deaths. It was almost a marriage of convenience and the chances of meeting other lovers rather remote. He always made love before going out or sending me out, as if that would cement us.

'You're orthodox,' I would scream, sensing the rationality behind his passion.

'It's called husbanding; it's allowed.' In many ways we were still strangers.

So to counter him, I wore my jeans ragged, and my T-shirts a little small, to which he laughed and said, 'It's clearly a form of elitism, to wish that you were poor.' I shuffled along and kicked pebbles and sucked nectar out of orange bell-shaped flowers. I picked up stray cats and littered the house with cheap fiction. He shut me out by listening to medieval music.

We travelled a lot, usually to cities near the sea, and Casablanca was one of them. Wherever we went, he spent the day in the library. I went with him sometimes, but I got easily, quickly bored. The silence and the dusted tomes disturbed me. So I spent all the while looking out of the window.

Later in the week, sitting silently beside him in the ice-candy pistachio-studded library building, I saw the pack of bodies on the sand, and further out, the oblong rough beaches undisturbed by tourists, where I wanted to go. Sensing my longing, Paulo sent me off to buy ice-creams and sit on the rocks till he had finished.

It was interesting really, that solitude, the hot Mediterranean sun burning down on the cold Atlantic sea. I jumped over the rocks, and watched the seagulls, the fishing boats with their white sails. I saw the crabs prod out of their holes desultorily and hurtle back in when they sensed my presence. The coolness of water touched my back as I turned to the mosque.

It was mammoth, like a large humpbacked whale, lying still and grey. Yet unfinished, it was being paid for by the taxes on the fisher people. The workmen were inside, and the light came in curious gauze patterns, grey shadow and gold in turns.

Harry Coonor was there, in his khaki clothes.

'What are you doing here, Mariam?' He was turning the knobs on his expensive camera, taking pictures for his book on religion in Morocco.

'Looking around,' I said, feeling the sand under my feet, and the towering grey concrete dome above my head blocking out the sky. The windows were large and it was still afternoon. We could hear the hammering and the blasting, the loud thud of some heavy metal as it came crashing down into the ground.

'Dangerous to be here alone,' he said, in the proprietorial way that men always took with me, as if I was undernourished or mad.

'Why?' I asked.

'It's a foreign country. You're not at home, you know. You don't speak any of their languages. You're unaccompanied. You're a woman. Any more reasons?'

'All right,' I said, turning away to go out.

He walked back with me to the metalled road where his motorcycle was waiting.

'See you when Paulo gets back. Tell him I want to discuss the chapter on maraboutism.'

'What's that?'

'Look it up in the dictionary. Why don't you find some other rooms, both of you. At this rate I'll lose my vocation.' He was deadly serious.

With a great roar of his motorbike he was off, his black hair streaming in the wind, his face sharp and white and tense, his nose jutting out like a crag. For a theologian he had a lot of money.

I met the girl soon after. She had brought in the shopping for her family on a little two-wheeler. She had a ponytail high on her head, and beautiful brown skin and black eyes. She looked thirteen.

'Want a ride?' she asked in English, seeing me watch her.

'Yes,' I said, involuntarily.

'Hop on then,' and she gave me the most beautiful smile I'd ever seen. 'Like to see the sea?'

'Yes.' I laughed as she shot-off faster than I could have imagined. The sea was there on the side of us, but the roads were busy, and there were so many flat bodies on the beach it was distracting.

'Got money?'

'Sure, lots. Why?'

'I get thirsty when I ride. What do you do?'

'Rich man's wife,' I said blithely.

'Ah.'

We rode along in silence, and then she turned into the crowded city, away from the beach road. I was surprised.

'Where are you staying?' she asked me, turning around.

'El Kandahar.'

'Biggest hotel in town. In the rooms on the side, with the little rose gardens, where you get crocus growing sometimes?'

'Yes.'

The streets were crowded. Women sat with market produce, their caftans billowing in the breeze; mountain faces, round like – yes, apples or the moon.

The smell of mint tea, brewed in fine white metal jugs, was all over, there was corn roasting on coal, popping delicately over embers, and figs strung in sticky chains, and blue pottery like the sort I saw in India. There were lock- and keysmiths, and boys with caged birds in many colours, French newspapers and delicate underwear in large woven reed-baskets, Egyptian cotton vests, snails boiling in hot water and carpets flung over balconies. There was orange juice with large seeds drowned at the bottom and mint leaves floating on top and music that tore out of shops. There was leather and silver for sale. A boy of eight stood in the middle of the road waiting to cross, and as we came toward him, he looked right into my eyes and shook his head. It was an encounter lasting a fraction of a second, but he said it, 'Don't Go.'

Did it really happen, that child's gesture of warning. Paulo often called me 'moonchild' because I could communicate with animals. My dreams were often prophetic – the moon could seize me and toss me if she wished without causing me harm. So I knew that that child – that stranger, standing on a traffic island, between the pigeons eating corn and the red vivid flowers of the desert, with the African peddler and his silver money pendants and bracelets – was telling me something. I couldn't go back and say 'What?' so instead I asked the girl, a little nervously, 'Where are we going? We've left the sea behind. I want to stop.'

She turned back, and suddenly I saw that she was not thirteen at all. She was eighteen or twenty, with smoke-creased dull stones for eyes. She didn't answer.

'I want to know where we're going,' I said again.

We had now left the city behind us, she turned right, out onto the main highway. There were a few people about, but the road was getting lonelier.

'Stop now,' I screamed.

'No. You stay. I take you to the sea.' Her face was so hard, her eyes so mercenary I doubted if she had ever known a childhood. Her skin gleamed like mine, but she was the stranger Paulo had spoken of. I thought of Paulo and the way he always asked of the tense nervous voices on the telephone, 'Is there a particular problem?' I would have loaned my soul for a day just to hear his voice at that moment.

I put my feet on the tarmac and I dragged it. I dragged with all the weight that I was capable of, and I was strong. All that brown unpolished rice, the different kinds of bananas, some a foot long which grew in father's yard, those flat white fish we ate at every meal, the raw green mangoes, those yellow ones with fibrous stones, those jack-fruits with a drunken smell about them which attracted tiny honey bees, those sweet ant-run coconuts had given me strength which didn't show. I remembered the citrus fruit which fell and pounded the roof. They were deep red inside, every cell like a jewel. I would spend most mornings at my father's house knocking them down, and eating them alone sitting on a fallen log, spitting out the seeds, waiting for the rain. I wasn't going to lose my life on the Casablanca Corniche. The tamarind pods would be bursting. They hung too high to knock down, and one had to hang about and look for them among the decaying leaves. We never burnt leaves. We let them compost. Some-one else a million years from now would be growing things. Father and Mother would be waiting for me and Paulo couldn't go back empty-handed.

She stopped. I quickly got off. She screamed at me in French, and I screamed back in Malayalam, guttural gen-etic sounds.

I started to walk back. It was hot, a four o'clock sun. I felt confused, frightened – not of the girl, because she was somehow ridiculous, a small recognisable stupid offensive sort of evil. It's when you're travelling that you feel the world is human: it's big, it's different, and you want to talk to people. Kidnapped in Casablanca. I could hear my friends laughing, and Paulo's silence.

I took a taxi back to the hotel, to the mountains of glass, where tourists were safe, and could hear 'Strangers in the Night' played efficiently on the piano in the lounge.

In the evening Paulo and I ate our couscous as quietly as usual, watching a beautiful woman dance while her lover played the most haunting music and watched her with passion and understanding. They were professionals and it seemed cold and fearless and not remotely erotic.

'I got kidnapped by a kid.'

Paulo looked up and frowned at me, drawing away for an instance.

fairer far in May

It was Father who showed me the lines on water melons. 'Look how perfectly nature has made them,' he said, as he cut a slice for me, running the sharp red-handled knife along nature's serrations. The seeds fell out, flat discs, brown and strangely hard, unlike the pale soft seeds of those other sand-coloured melons which had desert-rough surfaces.

When I walked through the market on summer nights I could smell the melons, ripe and hot, and I would hurry along past the cool fragrance of lime, mint and jasmine, for Father was now long dead.

Father had been so strange, so eccentric, that sometimes when I felt my blood flowing around my bones in steady circles I'd think 'Am I really his daughter?'

He had been very short, with big eyes, big ears. His only affectation was a perfectly trimmed French beard. He took great trouble with it, razoring the empty spaces every morning and trimming the rest with a small pair of gold scissors. Sometimes he would ask me to do it for him, and when I cut the microscopic hair around his thin lips it was with the same embarrassment I felt when he came out of the bath with a towel on and looked neutrally at the world in his own way. He would open his eyes very large while I cut the fine white hair, daring me to nick him. I never did hurt him though. His eyes were so strange, brown with blue rims which shaded into grey, that sometimes I stared into them, hypnotised. He hated proximity, hated touch, hated gentleness.

When he died, it was summer. The melons were out – large and green and perfectly round. We were going to have bitter gourds for lunch after the funeral with rice and watery whisked turmeric-yellowed curd. Father would have been amused by the solemnity of it all. He would have looked at the ringed and rough edges of those green bitter gourds very carefully, because he liked looking at symmetrical things before he ate them. I was hungry. I ate with a rapaciousness that shocked me but no one noticed because they were talking about Father.

I didn't like the memory of having sat near Father when he was dead. I'd never sat near him when he was alive. He didn't like us close – we stood at a distance and took orders. This closeness during his death was strange – that heavy odour of incense and this newly washed body.

I had no tears. They never came then or later. I felt it was a strangely golden day. Outside, the coffin stood against the mango tree where summer after summer he had hung a swing for us. The bees were heavy and full of nectar, and the bougainvillaea was drenched and rotting with last night's rain. I longed to go out, longed to stand at the gate and look at the field of sunflowers he had grown. I would imagine him watering the sunflowers with a bedraggled hose half a century old.

And then I saw my sister. She was standing at the gate.
'Father's dead,' I said, running up to her.
'I can see. He was ready to die. He wrote to me.'
Mother came, and she took Leah by her arm.
'Read the 121st psalm. It was the first psalm you learnt from him. Remember?'
'I will lift up mine eyes unto the hills.' My sister's voice was beginning to crack, tears began to streak her face in runnels of dirt.
'Can I go to the garden for a while?' she asked my mother.
'What's wrong with both of you? It's the custom to sit by your father. It's his last journey. You must sit by him.'
But my sister went out and came back a while later with the sunflowers. She put them on Father's hands, and suddenly my father smiled. I think it was the most beautiful moment in our lives, when Father smiled at us after he was dead.
We came back after we left him in the vault. I bathed in cold well water wondering if in death his many nameless and unspoken terrors had at last been laid. My thin and unformed body felt alive – it had all happened to someone else. I could smell bitter gourd as I scrubbed death odours from my body with the coconut fibre and sandalwood soap which Father always used.
I don't think Father was afraid of death. He'd faced it too often, alone with the angels, the avenging ones who'd come for his soul more than once and had been sent away by Father's look which always said to everyone, 'Don't come too close.' It was I who had to struggle now while I bathed in the captive underground water brought up in

a small metal bucket ringing up on frayed ropes clanging against the stone wall. It was I who saw his bereft sandals and looked alone for morning glories climbing up to the sun against the white fragrant flowers of the guavas. And the days that followed his death became heavy because I hadn't understood his death at all.

'Stop behaving like Mordecai,' my sister said, looking at me while I watched ants all morning – large, brown, with legs that quivered over the rough dark bark of the old lime trees.

'Who's that?' I asked, watching another ant entering carefully the dark hollow filled with rain water half-way in the trunk.

'Ashes and sackcloth, you fool.'

'I see. And what else am I supposed to do?'

'Father's dead, isn't he? You can't get him back. Now get on with living.'

'I can't,' I said, turning my face to her, so that she could see my eyes as still and empty as his had been.

'Scream then,' and she hit me hard on my back with all the violence of a childhood familiar.

The silences grew inside me, not for his absence – that I was familiar with even when he was alive – but because I couldn't understand the rotting fecundity of death.

Then one day, death visited me. I was asleep, curled up like a snail in its shell. It was afternoon, and through my sleep I could hear the rain. And then, when I tried to wake, I could not. I struggled. I thrashed. My body went into catherine wheels round and round. I could still hear the sea, over the sound of the rain, and then everything was still. As I lay there in that nest of absolute silence I heard the loudest beating of wings. How shall I describe it? It was loud and the wings were alive and the whirring and flapping became circular and smaller and seemed to enter my ear and all was once more still but in a different way. So that was death, when the wings of my soul could not re-enter but waited outside, beating like an eagle's wings.

That was death, and I was to become as familiar with waiting for it as Father had once been. I knew what it was – a quiet resolution of heartbeat and revolution. It wasn't frightening or lonely, it was just another strange experience. I saw Father smile again, and understood that flowers closed most days.

returning to dust

It was just a joy ride on top of a London bus. There were Samoans and Cretans, Arabs and Maltese and Americans and me. The colours of the city sped by, green trees, white Georgian buildings, square parks with red tulips and grey pigeons – familiar sights out of postcards and novels. I sat by the window just behind an Arab woman in a burka with filigree necklaces. Her husband, an unshaven handsome man with huge dark eyes, protective of his veiled beautiful delicate wife, held the baby.

I'd squeezed myself into a pair of cigarette-tapered jeans, and a loose white shirt. My hair had grown out nicely, lots of black curls with some silver threading through like an ornament. The jeans were uncomfortable. They made patterns on my waist, but the cut was nice. If I ate a chocolate ice-cream the elastic would snap, so it was going to be just chewing gum the whole day. Anyway I didn't have money for food today – my bus ticket cost me all of fifteen pounds. I hung out of the window and looked at the signs: 'Business is booming, don't let Labour blow it'. I sat back. Yesterday I'd wandered around looking at bookshops and clothes stores, and the loneliness and warmth of London – such a potent combination! –had caught me by surprise.

A woman with short snappy blonde hair, a string of pearls and a smile for everyone got in. Her gawky daughter who would one day be beautiful followed, and then her husband – tall, balding, hook-nosed, thin lips, no smile. He had to be from Texas. His trousers were shabby, his khaki shirt frayed. His wife sat with their daughter, her white smile echoing her pearls. The man sat next to me. He slapped his daughter's tawny knees, he grinned a little at his wife. Then he turned and looked at me, his companion for the moment. A shocked look, almost a jump, then he turned away. I was hurt. Yes, I'm black, so what? I thought it was old-fashioned of him to jump in that obvious way. Some days, some seasons I'm 'wheat-coloured' as we say in India, and there are seasons when I turn completely dark, when the sun burns my face and neck and all that's exposed of me. Then my body appears strangely patterned – white legs and chest, burnt brown midriff and neck and face. Sometimes when that part of my body concealed from the sun begins to turn white I feel afraid – I keep looking at the blue veins, some are green – and this sense of terror falls on me. I need my husk, it conceals what I would dread to see and hopefully the secrets of my body will die with me: I can't bear to think of my red heart, my purple liver, my pink lungs and my pale intestines coiled and whirling and pulsating inside like copulating serpents. Anyway, I was hurt that this man with his high leather boots and his fading clothes with the posh wife had looked so startled at seeing me. What could I do? My shirt was clean, my underwear new, my perfume came out of a turquoise crystal bottle and had cost me forty pounds. 'Daddy's rich and ma's pretty,' I started to hum softly, as my white linen shirt bellowed out into the London summer sky.

The man didn't stop breathing heavily. And then suddenly his shoulders touched mine, and we were breathing the same air.

His wife called out to him and pointed at something – some tower, some steel and glass frame, some cross. He nodded, and then he turned to look at me. He seemed hypnotised. His camera hung around his neck, and he didn't raise it once though his wife pointed and screamed with excitement. His daughter was content, and his wife adjusted her ponytails, and slapped her knuckles as she chewed her nails. The man didn't touch me after that, just sat with me. I felt my loneliness go away. I was sorry for the beautiful woman and the child, but somehow it was beautiful sitting with this tired middle-aged stranger. He seemed content too, and I realised that the startled look was not revulsion, not apartheid – it was just the opposite.

Being striking has its advantages specially if you don't want to exploit it or make use of it. You just sit in one place, and you get all the attention you've ever needed. I paint myself and it's something that gives me great joy – colours stick to my fingers and my clothes, and the brush feels hard and thick, hair of deer, of fox, of porcupine.

The golden-haired woman knew she'd lost her husband. I didn't want him particularly, but it was nice having him near, and in any case I knew she'd have him back. I tried to feel regret, guilt, but all I felt was a terrible nostalgia. It hung between us. He was loyal, patient, distraught, distant. Somewhere, along time's tympanum, I could hear his silent assent to everything I'd wanted, everything I'd been, everything I could be. He stood guard over me, he protected me, he wanted me with every core, fibre, cell, atom, node and orifice of his body, and yet would not touch me. That first instinctual shudder had been an echo, that first accidental brushing had been a test. We seemed to enter that thick fog together and then suddenly passed the Tower of London. The sky turned grey and cold drizzle fell on our faces and the woman screamed in terror, 'I'm going down,' and without looking at her husband she lurched down from the open deck of the bus, her white heels rocking dangerously, the soles of her feet arched and delicate. Rich people just can't stand the rain. The daughter stayed passively, while the man gave me one look and then, head bowed, held his child's hand and went slowly down the stairs. The four boys at the back, in T-shirts and cricket caps chanted intoxicatedly and meanly, 'OFF with her head! OFF with her head,' as we passed the Tower.

I wanted to get off but the absurd blue drawbridges were pulled up, and the Tower was drab grey in the drizzle. It was raining now but I hung on a while remembering the darkness and the damp, the dull beat of soldiers' feet, and eyes that smiled at me and then saw me die. He'd always looked for me, and that last look just now and the chanting of the boys and the shark's-teeth edges of the Tower pierced a hole through my ears. I felt dizzy, there was no one up there except the four mad boys swilling beer.

I went carefully down, my shirt clinging all along my right arm where the rain had slanted in.

The man and woman and child were still on the bus, warm at the back, a family again. The man's face was pale and none of us looked at one another. Everything was perfectly understood. The woman said, 'Black harlot steals my husband.' The man and I carefully said, 'Déjà vu!' – and not a word was really said by any of us.

I hoped not to have to travel with them. It as just so cold upstairs and there's always something mildly dangerous about beer swillers when they sit with their knees across the seat, their expensive shoes hanging very near you though they are sixteen seats behind. And they sing raucously. 'I'll get off at the next junction, and change the bus,' I thought. On a fifteen-pound ticket you could catch any and all the buses in London for twenty-four hours.

'PICCADILLY,' shouted someone. I got off. So did everyone else. The whole bus emptied out. We were meant to be herded into another bus. The golden-haired woman – she was truly beautiful, though ageing – looked at me in complete panic. Then she ran, left her husband and child and ran. Clack clack clack went the white heels across the cold grey wet slabs. Her husband yelled, 'SANDRA, SANDRA.' He was beyond himself in panic, the little girl holding his hand tightly, damp brown tendrils clinging on her forehead. He gave me another look, it was nothing – just goodbye. Then he ran after Sandra, who'd got into a crowded red bus waiting on the other side. He loped between the traffic, and got in just as the bus took off, hoisting his daughter carefully up the steps. Then the bus stopped again. Some of the passengers from our stand ran across. I could feel Sandra and her family staring at me through the glass panes. I had changed the metabolism of their existence. I hadn't meant to, but it had happened. They would forget of course, but something delicate had snapped, something irreplaceable, for the first time that morning I felt lonely, and it showed.

It was Piccadilly. I crossed the road, wishing to get lost. I sat in an Italian coffee house where they roasted the beans and ground them before you. It all took a lot of time, but the coffee was this-worldly, here and now, its acrid taste ground my dread and fantasies to a halt. I took out my sketchbook and drew the man, the child and Sandra, before they'd seen me. Then I looked out at the people crossing my path, none of whom knew me, or had heard of me, and cared even less about my past than I had in my childhood.

This double burden of reincarnational memory and my genetic roots – how grim it could sometimes be. In the rush hour, suddenly people stopped and stared. My face with its half planes and shadows, had been passed down generation after generation in a community which lived near the sea, so that we were born with pores ingrained with salt, noses strong as the prow of ships, eyes slanted and heavy as Buddhism passed our shores to Lanka. We were Christians by birth, sure, but it was Hinduism and Buddhism that clung to our epidermal cells, sloughed off in times of danger and protest against our otherness. Returning during times of peace, when criss-cross was allowed.

And then there were these other memories – translucent, iridescent, opalescent, luminescent – floating past, creating flesh from things once dreamed, once read, once lived, and yet so real.

I had it all worked out: death was a moment and then you hung out in a silence somewhere till you were needed back here. Heaven and hell were what you made happen for people – that was the power of being human. So, of course, one had been everywhere and done everything – and if one read Virginia Woolf's *Orlando*, it became simpler still, because the soul childlike and unchanging like a prism, a tiny diamond, reflected through its fragments the changing glitter of the sun.

Having paid thus for a moment's unthinking flirtation in the bus, I consented to have my portrait painted. I could paint myself well enough, but the street corner artists were poor, handsome, persuasive, Gaelic. Another ten pounds. No gifts for friends and family back home, that's for sure.

I sat on a small chair, while the small man with golden-rimmed glasses sharpened his charcoal pencil. I fell into a lazy dream. When I woke I found he'd drawn me so that I looked like Iris Murdoch. I adored Murdoch, read every line, but I didn't want to look like her. My face had lost its planes and shadows (or maybe I'd had them once?) and had fallen into this heavy middle age which he now produced on thick grained paper. I barely looked at it. I gave him his money saying bleakly 'very nice'. This hurt him so much he folded his chairs and canvas and shut his boxes with a snap. He'd taken three hours. I'd barely noticed. Art is an egoistic business.

I wanted to see Murdoch badly though, and the drawing was a reminder that sometimes intellectual pilgrimages had to be made. I wanted to paint like she wrote – all those small details, those light incandescent figures like Rain and Mor, those heavy embossed figures in *Bruno's Dream*, swinging across words like webs with the ferocity of large spiders, those waiting lovers out of medieval dreams, that perfect mismatched coupling in *The Sea, The Sea*.

I told Sunil I wanted to see him. I lay in my narrow bed in the hotel near St Pancras, where the bells chimed all night and all day.

I'd gone there early in the morning, and one of those lovely English women in tweeds had welcomed me and said, 'Please join us, we're about to begin our prayers.' I felt absurd, but agreed. What else could I do? She was anxious, eager. Christians were, it seemed, hard to come by.

We sat right next to the altar. I tried not to feel nervous. Christian I was by birth – but by disposition? There were three ancient women, two priests (one young and aggressive, the other soft and wise and old), the tweed-clad woman full of charm and personal eye contact, and myself. They sang a couple of hymns. I sat quietly, listening. Just then twenty-five Japanese students came in. They looked at the stained glass, the ladders and paint, since renovation work was on, the seven people near the altar. The wavering voices became stronger. Yes, they were singing 'Onward Christian Soldiers'. The children sat down. The church became full of hope – it bounced around. They had eager faces these lovely straight-haired children with their snazzy complexions and pretty clothes. Tourism fell from them as they listened to the songs, and somewhere invisibly, the organ played – loud and heavy, rich, lonely, echoing.

Bloomsbury was around the corner. I had woken up very early and gone looking for Virginia Woolf. 'Is Virginia Woolf's house nearby?' I asked a man. 'Nowhere nearby as far as I can see,' he said politely, looking about courteously, ignorant of women writers generally, and Woolf in particular.

The young priest broke my reverie: 'Today is St George's Feast Day.' Then he proceeded to exhort by the sword. The Japanese children walked out politely. A shade of embarrassment hung in the empty church. We shook hands at the end and I left, pleased to be out.

Then there had been the ordeal of breakfast: sausages and fried eggs. I'd gone past the sausages for six days and finally I decided I'd eat two. When I speared them, the fire alarm bell went. 'Oh no!' I thought. I have this friend back home in Allapuzha, who'd just returned from Belfast, who had told me about fire drills. I put my fork down. The other guests looked around. They were bemused. Most of them were small-town manufacturers and businessmen, film-makers, scholars, artists, playwrights. Unsuccessful happy people generally. The kind who wear check shirts and ironed blue jeans and smoke cigarettes. London on seventy pounds a day. The clanging went on. Nobody moved. What was the right thing to do? The Italian waiter, a handsome man with sleek combed hair, Count Dracula with even teeth, looked at me and at my sausages. He had served me for six days and he knew that I'd eaten cornflakes and toast and jam every day. He blamed me. I could see it in his eyes. He was from our part of the world, however modern his present incarnation.

Superstitiously he believed that it was I who'd broken some rule. I wanted to tell him, 'Hey, from where I come we eat anything which moves.' I was afraid he'd pass on his suspicions to the other twenty people bathed and eau-de-cologned in the room, so I got up and left. I stood out on the kerb. The alarm didn't stop, ten minutes gone by, and everyone in the hotel was standing in the middle of the street with the buses and cars going past to Tavistock Square.

Now it was not only the diners who were on the kerb. It was people who'd been bathing, sleeping, togethering in corridors and bedrooms. Many of them had come out in whatever they were in. It made me laugh. One man had a bag with all the valuables he wanted to fly with; women in dressing gowns, men with mismatched socks, some in very very little. And it was cold. The fire engine came. The officers marched in. The bells were clanging – theirs and the one inside. They came out in ten minutes. 'Nothing,' they said, 'No explanation. Some circuit went wrong.' The Jamaican chambermaid and the Italian waiter looked at me and exchanged glances. I didn't go back in to finish my breakfast, and after that St Pancras was warm, like the inside of lapis, which I'd just purchased from my friend who is a gemmologist. Then that episode in the bus with Sandra. And nothing to eat except chewing gum and coffee. And then painted by some Basque so that I looked like Dame Murdoch. I just had to see Sunil.

He was busy, but he agreed to come. We had been sporadic friends for many years. I'd reviewed his work – he was a sculptor and photographer often combining mediums – and he had reviewed my paintings, when we had not known one another. We liked each other's work, and when we did meet at last, it was warm, bright, happy. He was newly married for the last fifteen years. I found romance very exhausting, had never been married myself, but I liked him, and his being in London alone was charming and convenient for me. His wife and I were very close as well. She is a beautiful woman straight out of an Egyptian frieze. I suspect that the story that Cleopatra planned to flee with her children and servants to India (before her idiotic spectacular plan of deciding finally between immortality and obscurity took root) is true. Sunil's wife could have been a descendant of Iras, or some unnamed Cleopatrine offshoot.

'What's it this time, Eli?' he said when I met him in the foyer. He's astonishingly good-looking.

'I want to go to Cambridge,' I said.

'How odd, I was planning to go myself tomorrow. That's fine. We'll be off at eight. Don't be late. And I have to see friends so you do your own thing. And don't say you want to meet Murdoch. She's got Alzheimer's.'

The next day I waited at some station. Sunil didn't arrive for two and a half hours. He was wearing a shirt the colour of poppies and he smiled, waving at me across the crowds.

The woman who sold pencils and newspapers and chewing gum said to me, 'He must be really special.' I just bared my teeth. My knees hurt, and I felt horribly old. His youth and optimism got on my nerves sometimes, but there was a sibling bond between us, an understanding old as time. Syrian Christians are always tense about Nairs, brother–sister bonds and the attractiveness of the whole thing. The fear of incest is the greatest fear we Christians have, and then of course, adultery. Any moment one could stop being a Christian and become martial and polyandrous. One could lose the pepper trade, patriarchy, one's accustomed place in the Christian hamlet; a two-thousand-year-old genealogy can in a moment of ardour turn to dust.

'Sorry. I woke up late. And then the traffic jam.' He steered me carefully and avuncularly through the crowds as if two and a half hours of waiting were absolutely nothing. We didn't bother speaking in Malayalam – that made us both tense. It always had to be like this: platonic, brotherly, offensive, intimate. I was so enraged I couldn't speak. I looked out of the window and watched some really dull gold landscapes. I substituted it with fronds, water, hills, flamingos, brown-speckled ducks laying eggs in the silt. I ate figs I'd bought while I was waiting in complete silence, since I'd missed breakfast. I was afraid of the Italian waiter.

It was a perfect day. I can't describe it all. I'll just have to paint and camouflage out identities and warp and weave till we all become unrecognisable. What a pity! Because in itself such days do really happen, rarely happen.

We wandered for hours through the streets. We bought books and clothes and coffee. And then we went to King's College.

It happened as simply as a dream. I felt the heaviness of the chapel. I felt a lust such as I could not have ever imagined – it swirled out of the rosewood, it laid itself heavy upon my body. It was a concupiscence such as I would never know – of love and riches and lust and enmity all woven together. I could sense the heaviness of a man's body from which there could never be any release except through death, a cold, damp and spurting death.

And near me I could sense a different love, gentle, laughing, undemanding, familiar, boyish, light as summer rain. I would turn there instinctively, saying 'What?' and we would sit in the garden dreaming of nothing, waiting for sunrise and sunfall.

'Don't ever steal the past, my darling.' That brought my anguish to a close as I looked up and saw Sunil, his eyebrows crossing in a frown. Outside, pigeons sat on alabaster statues and tulips gleamed like childrens' candies.

Sunil disappeared to buy Body Shop body oil for his wife, his sisters, his mother, her mother. I waited patiently as he chose rustling dry rose scent for his wife and thyme and lavender what-not for all the other lovely no-longer-polyandrous Nair women he knew.

The day was not over. Iris Murdoch passed by. I opened my eyes wide. It couldn't be. She was in a wheelchair. She looked like an old Russian refugee aristocrat. And she was in a dream. Her face was round as the moon. Her eyes were as gentle as the Buddha's. She knew the world, and the world knew her and yet its passing by meant nothing to her. The boy who pushed her in the wheelchair was Adonis-like. 'She's lucky anyway that she has you who love her and serve her and understand her,' I thought. Directly behind them a slim delicate woman pushed a man who looked like a broken bird and he stared in passing at my navel as if it held within it the rim of the universe. For him life was all about star gazing and having seen them both, chairbound though they were, I could return to the gentle obscurity of my life quietly waiting for the rain to fall and the sea to rise in a far away small town in Kerala, visited by fireflies and shooting stars.

cleft

Soft slow tears floated down my cheeks and stuck on my lips till at last I tasted salt.

The only time this happened was when I remembered Mother.

I'd never met her. Folks said she was beautiful and that I had grown out like her though I was shorter and fatter. Sometimes I'd asked my father, but he'd get mad. 'Get off,' he'd shout at me, cuffing my ears even when I was big. Then he'd lock himself up and drink. I really hated him on those days, and so I found a simple solution: I never asked Father about Mother.

Just once, just once, I understood why Mother had run away. I was eight – no, maybe, five or six. I can't really remember. There came a beautiful man to our house collecting wild flowers. I really loved him. I took him to the river to catch a boat and hoped to disappear for-ever from Father's house, but he went away and never returned. I wonder if he remembers me. I liked every-thing about him, specially the round silver buttons on his blue cotton shirt. It had a Chinese collar. I thought it was a strange sort of shirt to wear, but my dad said that fashionable men in the city wore them. Then he blew his nose on his white mundu and unbuttoned his shirt and fell asleep. Father was the most crashing bore I'd ever met, but Elena says that like all Christian girls in Kerala I can't begin a sentence without 'Father said'. According to her most people in Kerala say 'Mother said', but we Christians always say 'Father said'. Elena is a painter and she's our neighbour.

Allapuzha is interesting. Such a relief to have left Father and Puthenkavu. My husband is in the paper business. It's either paper or pepper in these parts. If you're in fish then you're another sort of Christian.

I watch a lot of television. I like the films where you can't understand the accents and everyone has to guess at what the actors are saying. My husband (we never use names, not even pet names when we are together) reads a completely different story from me. The actors say completely different things to each of us.

Allapuzha is nice. The men sit in some shop, and the women have babies. I've got three daughters. I'm not sure when my birthday is.

My husband used to be in the tapioca business. He's been to college. He wasn't very serious, he says. Just wanted a degree so that he could marry in the right place. But then he saw me and felt that I would do. First proposal for me, and for him too. Thank God he liked me (with a mother like mine it's sheer luck that I'm married). I think he knew a girl in school he liked. But she wanted to make it in a man's world – write papers, attend conferences, travel and be an important person in the medical business.

We came to this town because his uncle who was a writer died of cancer and left him a house. His aunt didn't want to stay in it. She went to the Mar Thoma Ashram. She said that she couldn't bear the bigness of the house. She wanted to be in a place where people sang hymns morning and evening, and everyone fed the chickens together and milked the cows and chopped the vegetables and had Bible study classes. She knows the Bible by heart, so why would she want to go to more classes? Anyway it's her old age.

When he received the house my husband said, 'Oh good. It's the same town as Sara.' I felt really hurt. I didn't know who Sara was, he'd never even mentioned her once, and here for the first time I'd known him all these years, his body was singing.

'Who's Sara?'

'You won't know here.'

'But who is Sara?'

'We studied together.'

'In college?'

'Oh no. She's a doctor.' Then he went off to his shop.

I suppose she must be beautiful. We met once in the shop when I had gone to give him his lunch since the driver hadn't come that day. She had dropped in to buy paper and my husband said, 'Sara, we don't sell by the ream. We supply in bulk to paper companies.' She looked embarrassed and laughed and went off. Clumsy sort of woman, with very broad shoulders. A lighter fell out of her bag when she pushed her way past the rolls of paper. Smoker. No husband and father is now dead. I think she uses her house in the summer sometimes. I hope my husband and she are not lovers or anything. That would be horrible.

Like my friend Mariam, who went to Casablanca last summer and got kidnapped or almost. Nothing happened, really. But she did go off with a stranger, for a ride, for fun. True it was only a woman. And Paulo was so mad with her he didn't talk to her for a year. He just went completely quiet. He said that he had asked her to be careful when out in a foreign country. She told me that he wasn't talking to her or sleeping with her. And then it turned out that actually Paulo had a mistress all the while. She found letters from some woman and he said, 'Yes, it's true. I'm sick of looking after you. You're like a child. You have no sense. I need someone whom I can talk to, whose company is intelligent.'

I was really sad for Mariam. We grew up together, and I always thought she was so lucky to have a house and a garden and a swing and parents and a dog and a maidservant and books. I would have given anything to be Mariam. She called me Hana. It was because of her that I stopped being so wild and wretched. She loved me in a very sweet way. I told Elena about her once, and she said, 'Your friendship sounds mildly lesbian.'

'What's that?'

'Ask Philip.'

Obviously I didn't. There was something a little mean about the way Elena said it. She irritates me sometimes. When I visit her I feel a little afraid. She's always on the phone with those two other friends of hers. She probably knows Sara too. There's something a little similar about all of them. There's one who works on English lady novelists, there is another who plays a violin (sitting cross-legged) and I'm sure Sara is part of the group too.

'They're a lot alike,' I told Philip.

'Cousins,' he said, going back to his books.

Anyway it's enough that I *look* like mother. I have no intention of becoming like her, or these women. Mariam met her in Rome. When she left Paulo she went to stay with her cousin, who's a photographer also called Anna. That's why she calls me Hana. It's very confusing for outsiders that we're all called by the same names – Anna, Mariam or Mary, Sarah – there just aren't too many names. And last names, our father's names, tend to be the same too: Thomas, Paul, Jacob. That's it. But we all know each other so well, that we know who we're talking about.

Mariam stayed in Rome for a whole month. That was the last of her trips because after that she and Paulo separated, and she went back to her parents, and now she'll probably never leave Puthenkavu. It's a dreary place. There's just some hills and some rubber, and one river. Father had a lot of rubber lands. Philip sold them for me.

Well, in Rome, Mariam stayed for a few days with Anna, but Marcia (that's Anna's Italian aunt) said that Mariam was weeping too much and it was soaking into her limestone. Besides Marcia herself sweated too much while working (she's a sculptor) and smoked too much, and it was all rather ghastly for Mariam who was used to her own house: lace table covers and crystal, things I can only imagine, which she's told me about. So she couldn't stand it. She stayed in a hotel after that.

It was near St Peter's. Mariam took a bus from the main

station, Number 20 she said, and it dropped her at the Vatican Museum. She spent the whole day, imagine the whole day, looking at just the things on the ground floor. She said there was a beautiful woman lying on a tomb with hundreds of snakes coiling out of her hair. She couldn't move, she just stared till she thought she would become a strand in the goddess's hair, or maybe it was a demon.

I told Philip about it, and he said, 'That's Medusa,' but then he wouldn't say anything more. That's Philip. But he's nice to be with and if you do whatever he says, he's really very kind. And at least he doesn't drink. I find men who drink very depressing. Father – you should have seen him at the end. He wouldn't change his clothes, and got angry if you tried to change the sheets. Completely gone. Luckily he managed to get me married off, and stayed straight for just that one day. Philip's parents are very god-fearing. Whenever we visit them we all have to pray a lot. His mother's brother was a bishop. He died though.

Thank God for one's own house. We went to visit Eliyamma, Philip's aunt at the Ashram. There was a man who started shouting at us, 'The sin of Adam and Eve. That is the real sin. And you are continuing it.' My husband's aunt was very sad because she couldn't stop the man. Then she told us, 'All these people are very old. I'll come and see you. You don't come here. Don't mind what he says.'

Philip sends her bananas and mangoes and tapioca whenever he remembers. Of course, she never comes here. It's three bus rides, and at one point you have to cross by boat.

So I was telling you about how Mariam met my mother. She'd found a hotel near St Peter's. In the night she went to her room. It was a tiny cubicle of a room, but it had a ceiling which was very high, and from which hung a chandelier. Can you imagine – a room as big as my dining table, and in it a chandelier so huge that it had about three hundred tiny bulbs. It was the most beautiful sight in the world to Mariam, who had no home and no future. The hotel was once a bishop's house, and when they converted it into a hotel they cut it up into small cubicles, and she got the one that was directly below the chandelier. The light was so dazzling that she kept it on all night. She opened the window and let all the night come in. In the morning she felt she could live again.

Anna took Mariam to the airport to catch her flight back to India. And there they saw my mother Susan. Her husband's name is Zorba or something. Anyway it seems that he's very well-known in Rome. Philip says that I should see if I can meet my mother. 'No harm really, is there?' But I can't bear the thought.

Mariam said that Susan and she spoke to each other for a good half-an-hour. That Mother was very excited that I existed. She took down our address. I hope she doesn't visit us. It seems she wears Indian clothes. Thank God for that. Imagine if she dressed like Elena next door. Sometimes I die of laughter looking at our friend the artist. She came out yesterday with her entire back revealed. She walked down Stone Bridge in the rain wearing black pants and a backless shirt. People in Allapuzha are getting used to tourists, so they don't mind Elena too much. They just look away. Elena's pretty old and ugly, but once I think she was beautiful. Beats me, as they say in the movies. Why can't she act like she's forty?

There is a problem with all these women who hang together like those chattering birds – the seven sisters. I'll tell you what it is – they refuse to grow up. Perpetually adolescent. And yet it must be a different world. Well, the girls will be back from school. They're beautiful and Philip adores them. I'd better tear this up before he gets home.

ebbing

Susan left Azor at the airport. He had to catch a late morning flight to London. He stopped to buy some chocolates for her which she had stopped eating years ago. But she always accepted them with signs of pleasure. He kissed her, old though they now were, in front of hundreds of oblivious self-centred passengers. If you were in Rome you were there because life had come to a perfect circle. Christian or pagan, it was like a cool and steaming epicentre of the world. I must be growing old, she thought, flush or something. I wonder if it happens to everybody.

He let go of her but still looked into her eyes, touched her nose and mouth and wouldn't leave till finally she pushed him.

'Will you call me?'

'You know I will.'

'You should have travelled with me. It can still be done. I'll call Luke and ask him to arrange it. There's still a half-an-hour. I'll buy you some clothes right here or in London if you're going to say you haven't packed. Come on, it's only a couple of hours. Sasha, say yes.'

'I'll call you as soon as I reach home.'

'Where will you go from here?'

'Just downtown. I'll get home by evening.'

'What is downtown in Rome?'

'A couple of fountains perhaps?'

'I'll take you to Stonehenge if you come with me now.'

'Azor, it's the last call. You'll miss your flight.'

He laughed and hugged her and went off. His briefcase was frayed. She'd have to buy him another soon.

The kiss outside the post office in the airport reminded her of the first time it had happened. She'd sold her soul. And if she were asked to do it again, she would. It disturbed her sometimes that she who had been so good, so sedate, so well-brought up 'coming from an aristocratic ancient Malabar family' as her father had advertised long ago for her in the matrimonial columns, should have run away without a backward look. She was no Lot's wife, not even capable of pain like Karenina. What she felt for Azor and what she did with him was guiltless.

The first time he had come to their house (brought in by her husband, who was such a friendly sort of fellow), she had known that something strange and terrible was going to happen. The air had changed. His eyes were brown, dull, large. He was strangely emotionless as he looked at her. And she looked at his chest as if her head were already lying there. He knew what had happened before she did. His eyes wandered over her body shamelessly till she hung her head and went back to the kitchen. He was completely ruthless as he wandered all over, incapable of speech, incapable of responding to anything her husband said, and yet completely sane.

Azor was not handsome. He just communicated intelligence, passion, ruthlessness. She was used to her husband who was a suave gentle sort of fellow. And George had a perfect body, unlike Azor who cared nothing about being fit. Yet when Azor spoke to her later in the day after George's mother had fed them all, she felt she was swimming in his eyes. It took her a moment to disconnect, and to attend to the other things needing her attention. Like the baby.

Even then she had wanted to love the child, to hold it. But something in her was so broken after the baby. Nobody had told her it hurt. No one. Malayalam did not seem to have words for post-partum blues.

She had enjoyed the pregnancy. George had got her obscure things like oranges and chocolate. 'If you don't want to sleep with me it's all right. Mother says it's best we live in separate rooms. She doesn't want you to go home for the delivery. Says I shouldn't be away from the estate even for a day.'

'Of course, it was lonely. But it was all right with me. And the baby was as sweet as early morning flowers. But George was in a rush to get back to the State Rubber Board. I felt like death. There was no pain. Just a sense of doom, of being completely ironed out. And his mother was so anxious to separate us both. He was her pretty boy, her darling.

'And after that Azor just looked at me. I felt my world was trembling like a dewdrop at the edge of a leaf. It would fall in the earth and I would be absorbed forever. Azor showed me that life was exquisite, that pain could match love in a sharp and excruciatingly delicate way. He wanted me. And nothing stood in his way. "Didn't you have a will?" I can ask myself now.'

She sat down at the table with bright yellow umbrellas under a glass roof. She was talking to herself. How absurd. The water in the small crystal vase appeared intoxicatingly iridescent. She would get herself a drink, something fizzy and light. Go back home and listen to Dvořák and Greig.

Susan remembered the first kiss. He'd held her in his arms, bent her neck till she thought it would crack like a twig. He'd pushed his tongue into hers. She thought it was frightening, repulsive. She'd never been kissed. Married yes, but kissed? It wasn't customary. And George was so clean by nature, so fastidious. He always wore extremely white clothes, and washed his hair twice a day with soft bitter soaping bark. His mother used to get it ready every morning for him.

When Azor had finished kissing her in that ghastly brutal way, he rubbed his fingers all over her face. And then he was gone.

The next day it happened again. Mother had taken the baby to church with all those other ladies in white and gold, and George was away buying manure for the rubber trees. The fall was complete – but it wasn't a fall at all. It was complete and total happiness.

So she'd asked him to take her away. At first he'd said 'No.' He loved his wife, their child. This had happened because it had never happened before. It would never happen again because he lived in another city. He would never return.

She hadn't cried. She'd just looked at him till he forgot

his lovely effervescent wife and chose her. They just took off – no note. She never looked back, never really thought about anyone back home. There were occasions of course when the past was forced on her like the time when some anthropologist told her he'd stayed in Puthenkavu. She put on her glasses. She looked around. No one she knew. The day stretched ahead of her. Without Azor there were too many truths to be faced.

Before he'd kissed her that strange lonely day she'd noticed things appearing in the house that were not there. Small leaves appeared on the table by her bed. When she bathed, pressed flowers appeared on the still. Tiny cell-like formations appeared on the leaves. Dandelions floated into her room with her initials carved on the seed. She had started looking at things very closely. She began to pick up the leaves and flowers. Her name was on them. Written with some implement so fine, traced so finely, dried in a book, the dyes still delicate. Faint traceries of leaves began to fascinate her. Wings of moth and butterfly began to appear under her door. Again there was a message. Even if there was no message she began to look for them. The day did not pass without her picking up a leaf, a stem, a seed, a stone. The stones had chiselled hearts in them. Under the granite something would gleam: her name. And then his name. And so she knew it was Azor. They said nothing when they met every day. For Azor discussed his antiques with George who had a feel for bronze and rosewood. He would just look at Susan and she knew that while business was being transacted his eyes were on her – emotionless but questing. The openness and freedom of emotion came later.

With the loss of her identity arose a passion so steady, so terrible that she felt devoured in flame. These were clichés, but the world is lived, felt, experienced. It moves, provides new answers to the same question.

When Azor finally made his decision he stood by it. And together they had consumed one another in the endless cyclicity of the circle of snakes. There was no reason for her to mourn.

'Susan! Hello! Remember me?'

'Of course, Anna! It's been a year. We met at Marcella's party last year. You're her niece Anna.'

'I saw you with Azor just now.'

'I looked around hoping nobody would see us.'

'Well it's Rome, not Puthenkavu. Nobody minds if you kiss here. This is Mariam. She's my cousin. Coincidence – she's from Puthenkavu.'

'I keep meeting people all over Europe who say they're from Puthenkavu. What's your name?'

'Mariam.'

'And whose daughter are you?'

'Behnan's.'

'Oh I know Behnan. We were all children once long ago. Is Behnan's brother still as holy?'

'I've heard about you.'

'Oh horrible things I expect.'

'Yes.'

'Well, can't be helped. Here I am and not so wicked as you can see. Have something to eat?'

'Mariam's waiting for her plane. She's just separated from Paulo. She's going back to Puthenkavu.'

'Oh you poor thing. No fate worse than that.'

'It's all right. My parents are there. I studied with your daughter Hana.'

'I don't have a daughter called Hannah.'

'Anna. Anna George.'

'You know her? Really?'

'Yes, she's my closest friend. We didn't meet much after she got married. She was sixteen then. She has three children now.'

'Three children! Hasn't she heard of family planning? My God! Three children!'

'They just happened to her.'

'What, in a moment of passion? Or three moments of passion?'

'No, not like that. She says it just happened. Nature. She didn't want to interfere. She's a great mother, a really loving caring mother.'

'And I'm not, just an absent old woman. Never mind darlings. Heaven can't be had by all. Take care Mariam, and Anna, you too. Mariam, what's Anna, Hana's address? Give it to me. Maybe I'll visit her one day. I'm glad she's happy. Tell her I think of her.'

Susan took the address. She took off her glasses, dropped them in her bag, slipped the pale pink pearls out of her black shawl and was off with a wave. She had nothing to do all day, but she was completely ebullient that things had worked out so well for 'Hana'. She wanted to ask more questions, wanted to know so much, but Mariam's newly found grief, her intense love for 'Hana', all that was too much to bear. Six more hours for evening before she heard Azor's quiet breathing on the other side of the telephone. Some days he would call and say nothing. Then she'd scream 'Who the fuck are you' and he'd start laughing. The breeze blew into her short spiked hair. Her silks felt really good, swirls of them. Another twenty years with Azor till kingdom come. She just was not afraid.

water birds

The only friend that Mariam had when she went back to Puthenkavu was a woman generally known to all as 'Ammini beautician'. This was a thin angular woman with a long nose and thin lips and a giraffe neck who was a complete failure at her work, in spite of her shining knot of shampooed hair. Her failure lay in that she showed everyone how to thread their moustaches themselves and to step-cut their hair. So of course business was bleak. Ammini never knew why she sent away her clientele with the knowledge which, if kept to herself, would have made her a livelihood. People immediately presumed that since they had been taught how to do what they had come to have done for them they needn't return. Of course, the reason was that Ammini had a plantation owner for a husband, a man not particularly interested in love or death or money – he spent all his time reading newspapers. They used to pile up around him as he drank cup after cup of hot tea, for which purpose he'd hired a boy. Ammini's husband never told her that he'd been so madly in love with his first wife who'd died long ago that he'd lost his interest in the world in general. He'd married again because his parents had insisted – to die heirless would be a catastrophe for a plantation owner. But Ammini, beautiful and pliant though she had intended to be, found herself incapable of motherhood. She starved herself so that no child could be nurtured, and in the process made sure that her husband who was completely inattentive sexually would have no heir. Anyway, life had been so inconclusive that whatever happened to them was unimportant. She didn't hate her husband – he was too handsome for that. In fact, they looked curiously alike – their noses and mouths for instance were identical. It would have been a little like making love to one's brother. So they lived in a bored, but seemingly idyllic, companionship. She herself was not a great talker, but nor was she a good listener and for that very reason she had no friends other than Mariam.

Mariam was incapable of waxing her own arms or cutting her own hair, so in spite of Ammini's insistence that she could indeed do this for herself if she would but watch carefully, Mariam would return to the salon.

It was called 'Glamour' and it had clean white linen and everything was sterilised and polished. In fact, it gave Ammini more pleasure to keep the place looking ornamental – she even had orchids in the cylinder vases, as long as her own neck – than to actively attend to customers. It was more of a statement that she was a lady of leisure and had independent means. A facade, to hide the actual truth of things which was a desiccated husband drunk on tea and variegated news. She wished he had political ambitions or a passion for praying which most of the other clan members had. At the least, he could have visited his plantations. She wasn't remotely interested in his previous wife or perhaps they could have built a bridge on her sympathy and his suppressions.

In any case the parlour really had not too much of a function in a village where all the women grew and plaited their hair and saw no reason to put orange peel cream on their faces. It was not that they were all blessed with perfect complexion (in spite of the continuous rain). It just was not the custom.

So Mariam's frequent visits were rather extraordinary. Mariam herself realised that she was using some excuse or the other to go across. Sometimes it would be a shampoo. Almond crushed in egg or something equally exotic and awful. Or sometimes a face pack. It took away the boredom of living with her parents.

Her father and mother had been quite heartbroken that her marriage to Paulo was over. She genuinely thought that they missed him more than she did. She'd got used to being alone, really alone. Sometimes she cried and drove the car high up into the hills, stayed late till the thin silver moon came out, and the fireflies dazzled her. Then she'd return to heat dinner for her father and mother who would look at her with troubled eyes.

There was nothing wrong with Puthenkavu. It was the place where she had grown up, where she had longed to return during her travels with Paulo. As the only child of her parents she had always written to them every week – postcards with elaborate stamps of different hues which her father, Behnan, stuck on the side of his cupboard. He still had a collage of birds and flowers and humans from every part of the world. Behnan often looked at her with so much compassion that the tears would rush to her eyes. She felt that she didn't deserve the understanding that her parents gave her. They were, after all, besieged by questions whenever they went out anywhere. Why had Paulo not come back to take her? Was the marriage truly over? All that false and avid sympathy! There were days when, left completely to herself, she thought of suicide, but by nature she was too easy going to take her own life. After all, death could never be painless even if instantaneous. She could not imagine a struggle of that kind. When things got too bad she went to Ammini who got her tea, magazines, wrapped her in clean linen, combed her hair, talked pleasantly of the incessant rain. Ammini never wanted information. She saw herself as too serene in her captive existence to want to be hurled about by other people's lives. After all life had to be lived – one might as well do it with minimum decency and calm.

Mariam had once asked Ammini why she'd opened the salon.

'One must keep busy, my dear!'

'But you never encourage your clients to return.'

'Oh they'll come if they need me. I just don't want them to waste their money. This isn't Bombay.'

'But why have the salon?'

'To keep busy.'

It was completely illogical and yet Mariam could see that if one wasn't expected to provide companionship to a husband (or look after children one didn't have, or run a house with too many servants), a genteel task like running a beauty parlour would be facade enough to prove that one was busy and useful to society.

Mariam herself felt her jagged life take on a routine. Her room was just as it had been when she had left it, and she settled down into an adolescence that was vaguely familiar. She appeared when called, poured tea for her parents, chopped vegetables, picked fruit when the trees were in season. For each one of them their house had been the central principle of their existence. And though she had returned, the house took her back without regret. For so long she had been told that once married, she would leave, her mother holding her close saying 'Such is the lot of daughters.'

Now her mother looked at her with a strangeness, a sorrow that was hard for Mariam to bear.

'We should have chosen for you. I made a mistake agreeing to your wanting Paulo.'

'Well, he *was* a Syrian Christian. Nobody knew it would turn out this way.'

'His family has a history of instability. His uncle was a gambler, his grandfather a banker.'

'A money-focused family!'

'Don't laugh, darling. Your grandfathers were such holy men. On both sides.'

'I wish there were women priests. Then I could join Lukose Achen.'

'These are serious matters, not jokes.'

'I could dress in white with a crimson sash.'

'I'll see if I can buy a sari for you like that when next we go to Allapuzha.'

'And where will I wear it?'

'To a wedding, or a baptism.'

'I hate weddings and I hate children.'

'Oh, Mariam, it was just bad luck. We prayed but nothing could avert it. Your father wanted you to marry John Saar's son.'

'I know – the handsome physics teacher at CMS college. Oh well, I saw the world.'

'You would have travelled too – after all, everyone can travel. It's just that Paulo and you were always looking for excitement. You never understood that excitement comes rarely.'

'Well, I didn't want to stay in Puthenkavu throwing stones in the water. The only entertainment was to visit Chandanakavu. If you think crossing a treacherous river is my idea of excitement, it isn't, it wasn't, it never will be. I'm so bored here. I could die.'

'You were always such a good child. You were always happy. Now I don't know what to do with you.'

'When I was small you used to tell me to go pour water for the ants.'

'Why don't you?'

Mariam walked out. She decided that her mother's advice to look for ants and give them water was very sensible advice. It was a formula that every irritable mother had ready for bored children. How wonderful they were, those ants, always in such a rush. No blood, no bone – was it electricity that moved them? She wondered what it was like to be an ant – light as air, yet so completely oriented. She herself was so goal-less. Sometimes she dreamed that she didn't exist. That she was a dream that she had dreamed. Then she would struggle out of the knotted sheets stained by her sweat and thrashing and appear at the verandah to sit in one of the basket chairs that her father had specially made for her. Once he had found her breathing shallowly, leaning precariously over the balustrade. He had held her very close that time, and then – as if she were a small child – put her back in her bed. After that he put a fan in the balcony, painted the balustrades bright white so that they gleamed in the moonlight and got her the chair – a huge, wicker chair with an encircling backrest. She felt protected. She'd sit there with the rain and the lightning and the occasional moon flashing in, soaking in the steaming warm smell of banana, mango, tapioca and tamarind as they flowered and came to fruition. Life didn't seem so futile then.

There were days when it never shone for even a moment and the sky poured rain as thick as tears. Snakes floated out – large and spotted with white underbellies – and everyone stayed in.

There was absolutely nothing to do. Mariam stayed in bed on those days, hiding.

'Get up, Mariam.'

'I can't.'

'Go feed the goats.'

'I hate them.'

'I wish I'd spoken to Lukose Achen about this.'

'What?'

'Your fears. Your inability to live a human life.'

'I don't want to see Uncle.'

'I'll have to speak to him. I'll tell your father.'

'All right I'll get up. Can I have coffee?'

'We're making lunch. You should have thought of coffee earlier. This is my old age. And you're lying in bed.'

'Going, going.'

'I can't heat your bath water. Can't you find something nice to wear?'

'For whom?'

'For yourself. You're so young.'

'No one will marry me.'

'Why should you think of marriage now? You had your turn. Much use you made of it. Instead of having children you were gadding about.'

'At least I have something to remember. Not like you, who haven't stepped out of Puthenkavu. You don't even know what Ernakulam Station looks like.'

'Must we hate each other?'

'You gave birth to me.'

'And what good was that? Your father spoiled you. Even now he says nothing when you hide in bed like a bed bug.'

'I wish the sun would come out. Then we could have fresh dry sheets and I could do something.'

'Go feed the goats.'

'Why should I feed the goats? You sell them anyway.'

'We're not butchers.'

'Why should I feed the goats?'

'All your morning breakfast is wasted. Who's going to eat it?'

'We keep the goats so that they can eat what I waste?'

'Yes.'

Her mother left the room in such rage that Mariam started laughing. The fights were normal, inconclusive. What was she to do?

She blew her nose on the bath towel and then looked at the thick yellow clotted phlegm in despair. She went to the bathroom and tried to wash it off. If her mother saw her blowing her nose on the towel she would start screaming. Everything seemed to set her off. If only I could leave home, she thought as she scrubbed away.

'Wasting water.' Her mother was back.

'Just washing the towel.'

'Tears?'

'No, just dirty.'

'Oh Mariam . . . We have to change things for you. You can't go on like this. I'm going to speak to Lukose Achen.'

'Can I have coffee?'

'Yes. Come. I've made it.'

Achamma put her arms out, and Mariam huddled there for a while. She went with her mother to the kitchen. The size of it astounded her always. She was so used to the little cupboards from which they had functioned. Paulo always had expensive carpenters come in who had fitted in shining dark glossy plywood shelves on which he then placed his spices in neat gleaming rows.

This kitchen was cavernous. It was of beaten mud, hardened over generations. The fireplace had large copper urns out of which there arose the fragrance of steaming rice. Sunlight, smoky and dull, filtered through the windows. Green palm trees could be seen in jagged patterns through the ancient wooden grills. The cook, Shantamma, an emaciated woman, was breathing down the fire with a flute-like bamboo. The sparks were flying about creating a storm of ash. Circular pieces of tamarind were smoking on a rack above – when done they would be bottled and redistributed among various relatives – an integral ingredient in the flaming fish curries that were cooked here. Paulo had loved fish steamed with pepper and thyme, served with broccoli or asparagus. She had always been nostalgic for the red unpolished rice and the fish that they had at home. Well she could eat a lifetime of it now.

'Crying again,' Shantamma said, looking up from the red, blue and yellow fire. 'Crying again. Are men so important to you? Can't you live your life without a man? Can't you find something to do?'

'Don't talk to me.'

'I taught you to speak, and now you're telling me to hold my tongue.'

'What did you teach me? Crow, crow, where's your nest. That's all you could say.'

'Well, you have a nest here with your mother and father. Why do you make a fuss? Come, see this fish we've got in this bucket.'

Mariam looked in the old rusty pail. There was a ferocious-looking snakelike creature in the water. It had sharp scales on the side and a three-dimensional body, somewhat like an elongated rectangle.

'Don't put your hand in. It bites.'

'Is it a snake?'

'We don't eat snakes. It's a Kuri.'

'Kuruvi.'

'Kuruvi is a sparrow. A Kuri is what you have there. Its flesh is white and tastes like peacock.'

'You've never eaten peacock.'

'So? I can imagine it, can't I?'

'I don't want to eat this. Can't you make something else?'

'And what fish do you expect in the monsoon? An eel is what you'll eat.'

The snakelike fish slithered about in the small bucket, whipping its tail about like a beautiful ribbon. Mariam's tears kept dropping into the water creating minute disturbances. Some sand was settling at the bottom. The eel was looking at her with the cruel dispassionate gaze of a reptile. She distinctly got the feeling that it wanted to eat her. She tried smiling at the creature but it merely stabbed about in the water.

'Put a finger in and it won't return it. I heard your husband ate snails and octopus.'

'Yes, he did. Everyone did in Casablanca.'

'Khasa khasa. You go now. I can't understand what you're saying. Take your coffee and sit in the garden. Rain's stopped.'

The earth was as yielding and firm as rain clouds which have not delivered rain. She walked carefully over the heart-shaped leaves and tendrils of wild creepers. Her mother was talking to her Uncle Lukose. They were standing very close as old people sometimes do when their relationship is so legitimate that no one would dream of alleging anything.

'Hello, baby.'

'Hello, Uncle.'

'And what are you planning to do today?'

'Nothing.'

'As usual.'

'I'll have a bath. Read a book. Go to the beach. Write some letters.'

'Have you ever thought of serving?'

'You mean at the table?'

Lukose Achen laughed. 'Your mother does that. No, I meant taking care of people. Looking after people.'

'You mean social work.'

'I mean why don't you go and live with your grand-mother and look after her.'

'Oh no.'

'Oh yes. I mean it. It's time you did something useful rather than brood.'

'It's all my fault. I brought her up. She should know how to behave. I should have been more strict with her.'

'No one could be stricter than you, Achamma. You're not just, but you're loving. Anyway she can't blame you for her life. It's her life. She has to use it, make sense of it. What use blaming Paulo, or blaming you? She has to start thinking of what she can do for people. After all, if Paulo had been from our class, our status, we could have asked him to look after our lands. He could have lived with Behnan and you, these two would have had children, the name would have carried on if Paulo had agreed. But he was a modern man – too used to passion.'

'I thought priests knew only about one sort of passion – Christ's passion.'

'My dear. Go look after my mother. She will bless you.'

'But she is such an old crazy bad-tempered person.'

'All these things are part of our fate too. Old age comes to everyone.'

'She doesn't want anyone near her. She said we were not to live with her.'

'My dear, what she says and what she wants are two different things. If you offer she will accept.'

'Will you have lunch with us, Lukose?' her mother asked hopefully.

'What have you made?'

'There was no proper fish in the market. We have only some vegetables.'

'What about the Kuri?' Mariam asked.

'We can't serve that.'

'I won't stay today. I'll go and visit Mother and tell her that Mariam is coming to stay with her. Pack your things tonight. And don't bring any of those sleeveless blouses because Mother can see very well even if she is ninety.'

'I only wear sleeveless blouses in the house when it's hot.'

'I know you have them because I've seen them hanging outside on the line. All the passers-by have seen them too.'

'I keep telling her, Father, that she should hang them in the backyard.'

'But the only sun, direct sun, is in the front of the house.'

'It's all right. Just a joke. You're still a child for us. Anyway you'll be happy to know that Markose is back.'

'Really? Really? Why didn't you tell me earlier?'

'He's not the marrying sort, you know.'

'I know. That silly Sarah. Silly unloved Sarah.'

'We won't discuss it. Markose probably thinks of you as that silly unlucky Mariam.'

'Uncle, can you take me to see him?'

'If you promise not to trouble him.'

'In any case, I can't love anyone other than Paulo. It's just that at least I can talk to Markose. He doesn't expect me to be like all the good ladies of Puthenkavu.'

'. . . who have never been to Casablanca,' said her mother.

'I think I'll go before you start quarrelling again.' Lukose smiled at both of them.

They walked with him to the gate. He put on his bicycle clips, his black beard glistening with rain, and took off in the bright sunlight.

Behnan had come back for lunch and was eating at the dining table. The rice was steaming into his eyes, and the eel – now rid of its thick crustacean exterior – was floating, white as mother's milk, in a scarlet curry. He was eating hurriedly, his fingers burning, his tongue scorching, his eyes watering.

'I have to go back to the shop. The pepper merchants and the tapioca traders and the rubber plantation owners and the paper pulp merchants are all meeting at three in the Town Hall.'

'Traders, merchants, owners, what's the difference?' Mariam asked.

'Capitalists, all capitalists.'

'Can I come with you?' Mariam asked.

'Women not welcome.'

'Oh, Father. It would be so interesting.'

'Divorced. Now you want to be like a man.'

'But I've been all over the world and women own and run shops.'

'This one will die with me. I'm going to sell it before I go senile. The money's all yours.'

'I'm going to live with Grandmother.'

'You're going to live with Valiyamma? Brave of you. Did she ask you? Have you any idea how holy she is? Hundred times holier than Lukose. She's quite happy on her own and so are we.'

'Lukose Achen was here. It was his suggestion,' Achamma said.

'And did he hold your hand and say what a good wife and mother you are?'

'He did as a matter of fact. He blessed me.'

'Oh and why didn't he wait to talk to me?'

'We didn't know you were home. You always jump the back wall as if you were twenty years old. Why couldn't you come by the gate?'

'This fish is nice. What is it?'

'Kuruvi. I mean Kuri,' Mariam said.

'My goodness, are we that poor?' he said, looking nervously at Achamma.

'No. No. It's just that the fishermen have not been going to sea. The waves are treacherous. And you know where the trawler owners sell their stuff – Kuwait, Dubai, Abu Dhabi, Saudi Arabia. Of course, they don't sell it in Puthenkavu.'

'Don't tell anyone, will you, that we're eating eel. I'll go and buy some proper fish at Kottayam after the meeting.'

'Get some sponge cakes.'

'You never grow up, do you, Mariam?'

'I meant, for Grandmother.'

Her father hastily washed his hands and dried his face with a coarse towel which he then threw in a bundle out into the bush. Her mother went out and retrieved it, putting it on the bough of the guava tree. Her father and mother spent their days quarrelling, but somehow it was always a kind of sport. They seemed to spend most nights in the same bed, though earlier when Grandmother had lived with them, they had different rooms and her father had to actually cross his mother's room to come to his wife.

'I must have been conceived at dead of night, when Grandmother rolled herself into a cocoon in white sheets,' Mariam thought idly. 'Now, in her old age, Mother seems so infinitely desirable, so full of energy. Lucky things. To have each other, even if they quarrel all the time.'

Her grandmother's house was three hours by boat, forty-five minutes as the crow flies. There was no bridge over the river yet, though she had heard that there were plans.

Her grandmother was astonishingly irascible. When she was seventy years old she had said, 'Behnan, son, you look after your father's house. I'll go to mine.'

'But there's no one in that house. It's been locked for years.'

'Just so. Why shouldn't I stay in it?'

'But who will look after you? It's most inconvenient. I'm so busy here. Pepper prices aren't the same. Listen, Mother, sit still.'

'I've sat still under your grandfather's regime, under your father's, under yours, and if you had a son – thank God you don't or I'll have to sit still under his rule as well. I have a house, I'll go and live there.'

'And what about your rheumatism?'

'I'll hire a servant. And don't get me a gas connection and a telephone. I don't need them.'

'You're wishing yourself an early death.'

'Don't be a fool. I'm seventy. Death can never be early now for me.'

'I'll come and help you settle in.'

'That is expected.'

'I'll send Achamma and Mariam to stay with you.'

'Here I am trying to get away and you all want to follow me. I told you, I can manage myself. I'm not going to grow any rubber or pepper. Just some flowers so that my old eyes can rest upon them.'

'Are you sure you don't need glasses? Shall I take you for a check-up? Shall I call the doctor? Is Achamma giving you your milk?'

'Behnan, I'm not leaving because I don't have room here. You have been a good son in spite of all the beatings I gave you as a boy. You were always in trouble. Do you remember when you set the haystack on fire? Do you remember when you sent the kittens in a pail down the well – luckily they didn't drown because Lukose Achen saw you, and he rolled the bucket up again? What fights you got into! Not a day when you didn't come back with bruises. No, I'm not leaving because you don't love me or I don't love your wife and child. But now I'm old, I have a house in my name, why shouldn't I use it?'

'Go then. Lukose Achen will be angry with me and the whole village will laugh at me. What do you care?'

'If you care for me then let me go.'

Sailing down the still green summer water, the rains at last having stopped, and September come in with a hush and sigh of petering drizzle, Mariam felt almost sane. She remembered her grandmother leaving the house twenty years ago – ancient pots and pans stacked in the canoe, her folding chair placed in the centre where she sat, holding a large black umbrella with a handle, which when unclasped turned into a dagger. It had belonged to her grandfather, who had been a coconut merchant, very rich, and paranoid. His father had been a pious impoverished priest, but he had amassed millions. Then the war came, prices crashed, and he lost everything. Behnan had inherited a fraction of the old man's property. His mother had sold everything to repay debts. Lukose Achen had been embarrassed by his father's mercenary ways, and had shut himself in his monasticism while the scandal of his father's dealings (all above board according to his mother), his extravagance, the litigations rocked their household. Since his father never talked much, nobody knew how to handle the financial disturbances. His mother never spoke about it, but Behnan knew that if they had still held onto the house and the acre of land around, it was because his mother had business sense.

Mariam had hidden behind the row of boats on the water's edge. Grandmother hadn't cried, she had looked pleased. She had her Kalpetti – her wooden box with her two sets of white clothes at her feet. She was carrying a blanket which Achamma had given her. It was hot, and Grandmother suddenly looked uncomfortable at Behnan's morose expression.

'Sanyassa! Sanyassa! she bellowed over the water in her deep rich voice.

Achamma and Behnan started laughing. They had wanted to go with her, but the old woman wouldn't allow them. The house had been readied, a servant woman installed.

The boat swished and heaved, about to go.

'I came here fifty years ago. And I brought a dowry. Five rupees and a fishing net with shells sewn on it.'

'Oh Mother! We know Father married you because you were pretty.'

'Five rupees and a fishing net! You can't buy a mackerel for five rupees now. Anyway, I have my own house now.'

'This is your own house, Mother.'

'It's yours. Maintenance is all I have by your father's will. He loved me and I loved him, and I sold his property to save his name for you, but by his will maintenance is all that I have.'

'So are you taking your own house to heaven?'

'We'll see. I might leave it to Mariam if she grows to be a good girl.'

'Valiyamma,' Mariam had called. 'I am a good girl.'

'When you're big, and if you're good, then you'll get my house.'

'Valiyamma, can we come to stay?'

'Of course, of course.' The boat dredged itself out of the thick mud like a reluctant man from a woman's body and the boatman took Grandmother down the silver water.

And now, Mariam was sitting in the same boat going to her grandmother's house. She couldn't help laughing at the memories of that parting. Only Achamma wept because she was so lonely for days till at last, she got used to it.

'She's not even your mother. Why are you crying?' Behnan said.

'There's too much work for me.'

'Is that the only reason?'

'No, I liked her.'

'It's all right. She's my mother but I enjoy the peace.'

'You keep going in and out. You're always busy. You never have time to talk to me. When Amma was here we used to talk a lot.'

'Go and visit her and take Mariam with you.'

But Valiyamma had always made it clear that she only wanted day visits. She didn't want them to stay over-night.

'I'm too old to have guests. I can't look after anyone. I only have rice gruel and dry fish. So what will you eat?'

'Oh Amma, I'll cook.'

'But you go home after lunch. Behnan needs you.'

Mariam wondered what Valiyamma would say to her living with her and looking after her. She hoped that her grandmother wouldn't ask her about Paulo. She had heard that he was very happily married, his practice was flourishing, his wife was a successful lawyer who specialised in domestic violence. Battered wives. Strange, he'd never raised a finger. Silence and contempt could batter. How had it happened? They were so happy together. Could things change like this? Could he be solicitous on Monday, and bored by Friday?

'I hope it rains. I hope my heart turns to stone. I hope I never shed another tear. I hope I never meet another

man like Paulo. I hope Markose remembers me. Some-
body to talk to.'

Mathen the boatman and her childhood friend, said,
'Mariamma, you're talking to yourself. In English I can't
understand a word.'

'I said I hope it rains.'

'What? I'll get soaked again. It's all right for you, you
have an umbrella – your grandfather's umbrella with the
scabbard. There's not a man in Kerala who doesn't know
that umbrella. But I'll get wet.'

'We could share the umbrella.'

'Christian girl like you talking like a free woman.'

'I am free.'

'So you are.'

He was curly-headed with a beard, a Roman nose, legs
very hairy exposed to the water – he had a cut on his
ankle and he was barely literate. But they had grown up
together; he had married, had two sons, was perfectly
happy fishing and boating. Why couldn't she be like him?

'You're going to cry. I was warned. People tell me that
you cry all the time.'

'Today I'm not going to cry.'

'Say tomorrow I won't cry, and then perhaps it will come
true.'

'Tomorrow I won't cry.'

'Tell me where this man lives and I'll talk to him.
Nobody knows my sister better than I do. I'll tell him
you're sad. Two years have passed. And people say that
you still want him.'

Mariam trickled her fingers through the sun-warm
water.

'He lives in London and you're not my brother.'

'All right. I'm sorry I spoke.'

'It's all right. Never mind. Don't worry. It will get better. Tomorrow is another day. Things will improve with time.'

'Stop your chanting.'

'I no longer feel it. I have better things to do. I am going to make a new life for myself. Freedom is better than enslavement.'

'Mariamma, look, look! Water birds.'

SUSAN VISVANATHAN teaches sociology at Jawaharlal Nehru University, New Delhi. *Something Barely Remembered* is her first work of fiction.